**A crack** ̶ ̶ ̶
**enough t̶** ̶ ̶ ̶
**Owen ju̶** ̶ ̶ ̶
to the window ̶ ̶ ̶ ̶ ̶ ̶ ̶ the clouds had
become. He'd caught flickers of lightning a few times
during dinner, but now he could see the storm in full
swing, one of those impressive displays of sparring
lightning shooting from one cloud to another in an
endless dance.

"Afraid of storms?" Cal asked.

"I *love* storms," Owen said. Then with a surge of
adrenaline, he leaped from his chair to pull Cal from the
table and hurried them toward the balcony door. Cal had
such an amazing, *deep* laugh. "Quick, before it starts to
rain! I have a great view from here. Look." He pointed
to the gap in the cityscape between the lights of Nye
Industries and Walker Tech, where there was nothing but
*sky* and flash after flash of lightning sparkling in the dark.
"These are my favorite kinds of storms. Isn't it beautiful?"

Owen was so transfixed watching the skyline, he didn't
feel Cal's gaze on him until he heard "Breathtaking" and
realized Cal wasn't looking at the storm.

The heat filling Owen's face made it impossible to
acknowledge the comment. When he dared sneak
a peek, Cal had turned forward again, his face lit
intermittently by bursts of light.

They stood on the balcony awhile, taking in the storm,
the natural lightshow in the middle of a glowing city,
quiet but content in each other's company—until
another rumble of thunder heralded the start of the rain
showers and they ducked back inside.

# WELCOME TO

Dear Reader,

Love is the dream. It dazzles us, makes us stronger, and brings us to our knees. Dreamspun Desires tell stories of love featuring your favorite heartwarming heroes, captivating plots, and exotic locations. Stories that make your breath catch and your imagination soar.

In the pages of these wonderful love stories, readers can escape to a world where love conquers all, the tenderness of a first kiss sweeps you away, and your heart pounds at the sight of the one you love.

When you put it all together, you find romance in its truest form.

Love always finds a way.

*Elizabeth North*

Executive Director
Dreamspinner Press

# Amanda Meuwissen

# A MODEL ESCORT

DREAMSPUN DESIRES

PUBLISHED BY

DREAMSPINNER
PRESS

Published by
DREAMSPINNER PRESS

5032 Capital Circle SW, Suite 2, PMB# 279,
Tallahassee, FL 32305-7886 USA
www.dreamspinnerpress.com

This is a work of fiction. Names, characters, places, and incidents either
are the product of author imagination or are used fictitiously, and any
resemblance to actual persons, living or dead, business establishments,
events, or locales is entirely coincidental.

A Model Escort
© 2019 Amanda Meuwissen.
Editorial Development by Sue Brown-Moore.

Cover Art
© 2019 Bree Archer.
http://www.breearcher.com
Cover Design
© 2019 Paul Richmond.
http://www.paulrichmondstudio.com
Cover content is for illustrative purposes only and any person depicted
on the cover is a model.

Paperback ISBN: 978-1-64108-096-5
Digital ISBN: 978-1-64080-694-8
Library of Congress Control Number: 2018938135
Paperback published March 2019
v. 1.0

Printed in the United States of America

This paper meets the requirements of
ANSI/NISO Z39.48-1992 (Permanence of Paper).

**AMANDA MEUWISSEN** is a primarily gay romance writer, as well as Marketing Operations Manager for the software company Outsell. She has a Bachelor of Arts in a personally designed major from St. Olaf College in Creative Writing, and is an avid consumer of fiction through film, prose, and video games. As author of the paranormal romance trilogy *The Incubus Saga*, young adult novel *Life as a Teenage Vampire*, the novelette *The Collector*, and superhero duology *Lovesick Gods* and *Lovesick Titans*, Amanda regularly attends local comic conventions for fun and to meet with fans, where she will often be seen in costume as one of her favorite fictional characters. She lives in Minneapolis, Minnesota, with her husband, John, and their two cats, Helga and Sasha (no relation to the incubus of the same name), and can be found at www.amandameuwissen.com.

To Jim—I doubt I would be here or anywhere without the chance you gave me.

## *Chapter One*

**EVERYTHING** had a pattern. The trick to understanding the data was in the models. The algorithms. The points along a timeline that indicated the probability of what should come next.

Owen's whole world revolved around patterns, but some things couldn't be predicted. Whenever that happened, he thought back to something his mother once told him.

"Meet every surprise in life like you had a plan all along."

Owen did not have a plan.

Looking around his apartment, he realized he also didn't have furniture. He remembered the moving-without-furniture part of coming to a new city; he'd just forgotten how annoying living without it would be until he went out and bought something. All he had right now were boxes filled with clothing, electronics, kitchenware, and keepsakes.

He sat on one of the larger boxes amid the clutter, facing the wall of floor-to-ceiling windows that led out to his balcony. The view beyond was humbling, a dozen stories up to look upon the glittering lights of the city, nestled in the heart of it. Owen had always loved cityscapes more than trees. He'd dreamed of having an apartment like this someday, and finally he had a job that let him afford it. He'd just hoped he'd be sharing it.

He never was good at new beginnings. He had to be out of his mind to pick up and move three hundred miles from home just to escape his ex.

Not that Harrison was the only reason Owen chose Atlas City. The mayor himself had offered Owen a consultation position while his new predictive models were put into use at the police department. One of the stipulations Owen had on any private or government organization using his patents was his personal involvement in implementation. Mayor King had agreed and brought Owen in to work part-time at the mayor's office while things got up and running. The move to Atlas City also opened doors for him at Walker Tech and Nye Industries to sell his models for industrial use. He'd never want for anything again with the opportunities and money headed his way.

For now, the ACPD would be using the algorithms he'd created to predict where criminal activity was most likely to occur, allowing them to position officers more efficiently and maximize coverage on the streets. Owen's models would save the city millions by better utilizing their current resources, and maybe even help save lives. It was everything he'd ever wanted, and if things went well here, his models could help even more people all over the country.

He should have been happy. He should have been ecstatic. But a shadow hung over him because of how things had ended with Harrison back in Middleton.

Habit caused Owen to wrap his fingers around his forearm. The bruises were gone now, no lasting damage, but sometimes it was like phantom pain when he thought about his ex. The older man he'd dated for years, who he'd lived with for years, who he'd believed would be the last person he ever came home to, had never physically harmed him until that night. Harrison's abuse had been different, deeper, if not as visible as the bruises once were.

The sound of Owen's ringtone startled him, sitting alone in the dark of his mostly empty apartment. He scrambled to remember where he'd put his phone before realizing it was in his pocket.

"Hello?"

"Uh-oh. Don't tell me the moving company lost something? You sound about two seconds from having a pint of Häagen-Dazs for dinner again."

*Alyssa.* Owen's sister had an uncanny knack for knowing exactly when he needed to hear her voice, ever since he was adopted into her family when he was ten.

Despite himself, he smiled. "I resent that stereotype."

"I would too if I hadn't caught you doing it multiple times before you moved."

They shared a chuckle, though the memory of how true that was turned Owen's expression sour.

The night he left Harrison, he could have gone to his adopted father, but Doug had never approved of the relationship.

"He's twice your age!" was the common complaint.

He wasn't *twice* Owen's age, though close, since Owen had been twenty-one when they met and Harrison thirty-eight. That was four years ago, putting his "boyfriend" in his forties now, which shouldn't have mattered, but Doug never let it go. He meant well, loved Owen like flesh and blood and had always been there for him, but sometimes that displayed as the classic overbearing father figure. Now Doug could finally say "I told you so."

At least he'd never actually said that. Still, Owen hadn't wanted to deal with Doug's judgment, so he'd gone to Alyssa instead. Her husband, Casey, was one of Owen's closest friends. They understood, but it was still awkward being a third wheel in their home for months before the call to Atlas City came.

Owen needed a change. He just hoped he hadn't made a terrible mistake all because a bad breakup made it too difficult to stay in his hometown.

"I'll get something substantial once I gather enough will to leave this box," he said, patting the side of it so Alyssa could hear the thumps over the phone. "Like Thai food or pizza."

"Owen…."

"Hey, I don't have any dishes unpacked yet. Or food in the fridge. Or furniture, for that matter."

"I told you not to let Harry have everything in the divorce."

"It wasn't a divorce." Owen scowled. All his friends referred to it like that, which only made the loss feel worse, because he'd always wanted to get married someday. He still did. He just hated the idea of starting from square one. "And I didn't want his things."

"Some of it was your things."

"None of it was mine, Lys. He chose everything in that apartment. It was always his, never mine, never *ours*. And I'm not completely devoid of amenities. I have a bed."

"You have a mattress," she said, just as Owen looked to his left through the bedroom door to see it resting on the floor like some minimalist mockery. "*My* mattress that Casey and I gave you so you wouldn't be sleeping on the floor tonight. You still need a bedframe, dresser, table—"

"I can't think about that right now. I'm meeting the mayor tomorrow and all my new contacts. I probably won't even sleep. I'll worry about furniture after work tomorrow."

"How about you worry tonight?"

"Lyssa…."

"Relax, O. Check out the large kitchen box I helped pack."

Perking up from where he sat, Owen scanned the apartment until he spotted the larger of his boxes labeled KITCHEN. "What did you do?" he asked as he headed toward it, expecting balloons or confetti to explode out the top in some lame attempt to make him smile, which honestly might have worked, but Alyssa was using her serious, practical tone. She couldn't be hiding an entire apartment full of furniture in that box.

Only somehow, she was—a catalog full.

On the very top was a catalog for an express delivery furniture store that included rentals. Even from the cover, Owen could tell the furniture was more his style than anything Harrison had ever allowed. Owen liked color and character and light; Harrison was too rigid for that.

"This stuff looks…."

"Amazing?"

"Expensive."

"Considering how much they're paying you, nothing is out of your price range right now. Indulge a little. Plus, this way you can relax and choose some things you like tonight, make the order online, and have everything delivered tomorrow while you're at work. If you fall in love with something, you can buy it. If you hate a piece once you see it, you can return it and get something new. I dog-eared pages of things I thought you might like."

Owen was already flipping through and came upon a dog-eared page as she said that. There was a small kitchen table with four chairs, each a different color— red, blue, yellow, and black. Harrison would have hated the asymmetry, which meant Owen immediately wanted it.

"You are the best, Lys."

"I know. Casey and I miss you already. Dad's holding up okay but still grumbling about you moving *thousands* of miles away—his words, no matter how many times I tell him it's a simple day trip in the car or a quick flight."

"I hope he's not too mad. Four years of Harry keeping me secluded, barely spending time with you guys or any of my friends, now just when we'd started to reconnect, I moved away. Maybe this was a bad idea...." He looked around the apartment again, feeling small and suffocated by so much space and so many miles between him and the closest people who loved him.

"Owen, Dad will get over it. This is important to you, something you've always wanted, the project you've been working on since you were a kid, and the one thing Harry wasn't able to twist into one of his own patents."

"Because I kept it from him."

"You weren't the bad guy. If you'd shared those models with Harry, he'd be the one getting cozy with Atlas City elite tomorrow. Instead, it's you, like you deserve, like you've earned. Don't run scared yet. This will be so good for you. But if you start to go out of your mind and feel too homesick, I'll be on the first plane there."

Owen smiled as he dropped into a cross-legged position on the floor to keep paging through the catalog. "Thanks, Lys. I can do this. It just doesn't feel like home yet with only boxes around me. I'll order dinner and have fun picking out furniture. Once I have the place decked out, I'll send pictures. Deal?"

"Deal."

"Hey." He frowned, reaching another dog-eared page, but this one had a business card stuck in the crease. "What's this?"

Alyssa had been the biggest asset in helping Owen move, from finding the right apartment to hiring the moving company. She'd even made him lists of restaurants to check out, corner stores in his neighborhood for when he needed groceries, and random activities to try so he wouldn't sit at home doing nothing when he wasn't at work. She was a good sister and a loyal friend.

But finding the business card made Owen question all of that.

"*Alyssa*." He balked. "You got me a referral for an *escort service?*"

"Hear me out—"

"I don't need to *hire* someone—"

"I'm not suggesting you do! I just thought it might be easier to have someone on standby for dinners and events if you weren't ready to date yet and didn't feel like answering questions about your love life. An escort could take the heat off, that's all."

Calming at her logic, Owen tried not to get too worked up over the implications. The card was sleek navy with silver writing, just the name, a website, and a phone number. "But isn't like... sex implied?"

"Not legally."

"Lyssa!"

"Nothing is implied, O. Is it easier for people to look the other way if sexy times go down, yes"—he cringed at her word choice—"but that doesn't mean there's obligation on either side. Some people really do hire escorts to *escort* them. Not that I'd judge if you needed more than that—"

"The last thing I need right now is mindless sex. That's all I was to Harry. His little trophy. Convenient and obedient. I'd rather have someone around who'd hold me. Oh God." He tipped back into a slow fall, stretching his legs out in front of him when he landed. "I sound like a failed greeting card."

"Owen." Alyssa giggled before shifting to earnest understanding. "Everyone needs different things at different points in their lives, and no need is more or less valid than another. I wish I could be there to hug you, honey. I really only meant the referral as an option for social events, no bad joke or pressure involved. You can totally ignore it."

"Sorry, I'm not upset," Owen said, staring at his ceiling. "It makes sense. I didn't even think about social events. I do not want to have any real dates right now, but having the option to skip the 'so are you seeing anyone?' conversation would be such a relief. Divulging that I just got out of a long-term relationship would probably make me someone's 'project' and they'd start setting me up with their neighbor's cousin's roommate and... urg, maybe I will call that agency."

Alyssa giggled again, but lovingly not mocking. "First dinner and furniture."

"Right. Dinner. Furniture. Disaster of a love life. That sounds like the right order."

After another shared chuckle, she said, "It's going to be okay. You're moving on. You're heading in a new direction all for you. You are so much more than Harrison Marsh."

That's what Owen had been telling himself for months. He knew in his bones it was true; he'd proven how successful he could be all on his own. He just wished being on his own wasn't so lonely. "I know. Give my love to Casey. I'll check in with you guys soon."

"You better. I love you, O."

"Love you too, Lys."

Lurching into a sitting position again, Owen hung up the call and stuck the business card back in the catalog as he continued paging through it. He couldn't imagine calling some stranger to be his date for whatever fancy event the mayor might drag him to, but the idea wasn't completely ridiculous. He'd barely dated anyone before being caught in the whirlwind of Harrison Marsh. He probably did need a professional at this point.

But no, he doubted he'd drum up enough courage to call an *escort*, though he did like the agency's name and implied speed in an emergency. If he ever got truly desperate, he had the option to call *Nick of Time Escort Service* to save him.


**NICK** of Time Escort Service. How may I help you?" Daphne the receptionist answered the phone as Cal passed her desk.

He hated coming into the office. While his name, photograph, and basic stats like height and age were all displayed in the agency's online catalog, places of business that relied on anonymity for their clients tended to not have office hours open to the public. Payroll, the receptionist, and any handlers had office hours. Cal's hours rarely included *offices* and were even more seldom during the day.

This morning, he had a bone to pick with the CEO.

"Mr. Mercer, may I help you with something?" Richard Raine Williams III, who Cal not so affectionately called *Dick*, barely glanced at the door when he stormed into his office. Daphne used to try to dissuade him from barging in unannounced, but she'd learned to let forces of nature run their course.

"Merlin's on my schedule again," Cal said as he planted himself in front of Dick. "I dropped him last week."

"And you are well within your rights to do so. However"—the Englishman flicked his eyes up from his computer screen—"if you would like someone removed from your calendar, you need to go through the proper channels to dismiss that client and work through scheduling and accounts. When you do not, the chain of command is interrupted and someone spends several wasted minutes on changes they might have avoided."

"Like *me*?"

"I was going to say Kendra in Accounts." Dick's insufferable deadpan irked Cal like few things could. "But I realize your time is more precious than the rest of ours."

Crossing his arms over his tailored suit, Cal stood his ground. His greatest selling point to clients was his precise nature—not to say his looks weren't an asset. "Don't bullshit me, Dick. I told Lara I was dropping him. Shouldn't the paperwork be her responsibility?"

"It is. You still need to sign it. And put something in the dismissal report other than you get a 'bad feeling' about him."

Cal thought back to his latest encounter with *Merlin*—a man of sizable means and expensive tastes, recently forty, dripping with poise and sarcasm, much like Cal himself—and grimaced. "It's a *feeling*. What more is there to explain? Have my instincts ever been wrong?"

The continued stare from Dick proved he hadn't forgotten the clients Cal had demanded the agency dismiss in the past, and not always because they were *his*, who'd turned out to be unsavory for one reason or another. "No, but rather than cut ties with Mr. Merlin outright, I would like to give other escorts the opportunity—"

"I wouldn't recommend that."

Dick sighed, but Cal was not going to budge. Atlas City was large enough that the agency could afford to drop rich assholes like Merlin without missing any quotas. Cal had never had trouble with the man. He treated him well, carried on a good conversation, followed the rules when things got intimate, but Cal couldn't shake the feeling that something was funny about him.

"Get him off my schedule, and *off* the roster."

"Of course, Mr. Mercer," Dick conceded. "Comfort for my escorts first and foremost, always."

He meant it, Cal never doubted that, which was the primary reason he remained loyal to the agency and always would, even when the rest of the time the CEO was a prick. "Thank you." Turning briskly, he made to take his leave.

"And do fill your vacant spot within the next few weeks, if you would. We are getting a bit full up. Perhaps you'd consider taking on a new regular."

Cal bristled as he reached the door and shot an icy expression over his shoulder. "I'll see what comes up."

*Nick of Time* allowed their escorts to vet and refuse anyone who chose them for a night—especially if a night turned into a regular occurrence. The client wouldn't be told they were refused, just that the escort was unavailable. Cal had a full schedule of regulars and very rarely took on new clients. He was picky about who he spent his time with, especially if that involved joining someone in bed, and it always did where work was concerned. He didn't take clients only looking for arm candy; he knew where his strengths lay.

The healthcare for *Nick of Time* was bar none as well, and clients had to go through an approval process with up-to-date medical records just like the escorts. After being accepted onto the roster, clients could have first pick of who they wanted for a night, though they were encouraged to choose second and third options since first-choice escorts were often popular and already booked. If an escort was fully stacked for their schedule, they were removed from the catalog until they became available again, but the final decision always came down to whether the escorts themselves were willing to accept who'd chosen them.

Still, there had been times when Cal agreed to see a client, saw them for a night, but even though the man or woman desired his company in the future, he deemed them unfit to become a regular. He'd kept Merlin on his calendar for far too long.

Making a quick left out of Dick's office, Cal headed for his handler—Lara Tyler. In a pinch, she was more bodyguard than secretary, but that part of her resume wasn't on the books. Cal had never used her services in that regard, but a few escorts had, and the stories they told were part of why so many gifts and flowers stacked up on her desk come Christmas.

Cal's mouth was already open in preparation to speak when he rounded the corner into her office and was interrupted by a stack of papers being smacked against his chest. He coughed as he looked down at the well-manicured hand attached to them.

"Those would be the forms I neglected to sign?"

"What gave them away?" Lara said with mild scorn bleeding through her smile—a deadly smile, made all the deadlier with red lips framed by a pretty face. Lara would have made an excellent escort herself, not that many people would dare tell her that. "I'm assuming you already gave Richard an earful?"

"What can I say, I hate the bureaucratic side to the job," Cal said, accepting the papers and following her to the desk. "I prefer to be more… hands-on."

Unmoved by the waggle of his eyebrow, Lara pushed a pen at him next, said "Put your hands to work with this then, Calvin," and spun her computer to face her while she perched on the corner of her desk. "Need an updated schedule with Merlin removed?"

"Please." He started to peruse his paperwork; it was a very thick stack in his opinion.

"Piper's back from vacation. Wondered if you could pencil him in tonight."

"Gladly." The client Cal had dubbed Piper because he played principal clarinet in the Atlas City Philharmonic tipped well and was easy to please with the right praises for his playing and condescending talk about the art his parents bought that he therefore despised.

Cal loved art and music, and Piper, while young, was worthy of every bit of praise Cal had ever given him. But much of high society, which was the majority of Cal's clients, revolved around trash masquerading as treasure, and that he couldn't stomach.

"Also, Prince had to reschedule for Wednesday. With Merlin out, you're free that day, so I gave her a maybe."

"You can confirm. Have you seen Rhys around—"

"Where's my damn bonus, Tyler?" A booming voice preceded one of Cal's dearest friends and fellow escort, Rhys Kane. He could slap on the charm on a dime and be whatever a client wanted, but he was surly and blunt when himself. Cal found it refreshing.

"Your referral bonus will be in the next paycheck, Rhys. I told you," Lara said. "End of the month."

Rhys grumbled. He stood a good inch taller than Cal's six-foot-one and was nearly twice as broad. His larger, muscled form attracted a narrower group of clients, but he was never without a full schedule. "I should get a bonus straight from Johnny for this one. You shoulda seen his face comin' back from his first night with this chick." He smirked at Cal. "I think the poor sap's in love."

"What'd he dub her?"

"Jane."

"Bit dull, isn't it?" Cal frowned.

"Like *Tarzan* and Jane. Apparently, she's got a thing for safaris, and you know how Johnny likes to travel."

"*Rhys*," Lara interjected. "We aren't a matchmaking service. Stop setting up referrals with ulterior motives to knock out your competition."

"Who's got ulterior motives?" Rhys shrugged. Johnny wasn't as large as Rhys but he did fill a similar demographic, and several past escorts had quit after Rhys handed them referrals. Rhys swore it was coincidence, but sometimes Cal wondered. "I just figured she'd like the guy, so I passed her his card at a party. That's what referrals are for. Whadda you got goin' on?" He returned his attention to Cal.

"Piper and Prince this week."

"Merlin too?"

"*Out*," Cal said, signing his name with a flourish on the last page.

"'Bout time," Rhys huffed.

"You've never even met the man," Lara said, taking back the signed forms and her pen.

"Cal's word's good enough for me."

Shaking her head at them, Lara set the papers in her outbox. "You know how Richard frowns on this shop talk."

"That's why we use codenames for clients," Cal said. "All in good fun. No identities lost."

"Why do ya call him Merlin again?" Rhys asked.

"Coz he's a magician, Rhys. I can never figure out his secrets." With most of the day free and his evening newly planned, Cal decided to make the most of running into his friend. "Breakfast?"

"You're on, pal. But till I get that bonus"—he poked Cal pointedly in the shoulder—"yer buyin'."

Cal expected as much. Heading out of the office, he turned to say his farewells to Lara, but she was already in front of him, pressing another paper to his chest—the schedule he hadn't noticed her print.

"Since you prefer 'hands-on,'" she said, even though she'd email and text it to him later. "But next time... paperwork first."

"Yes, ma'am," Cal said with a bow. "You know, you don't rag on Rhys about these things."

Lara's eyes always had a sparkle of danger in them, especially when she was in the right. "Don't let the loud bark fool you, Calvin. Rhys is the most reliable one of the whole bunch."

"But I'm still the most popular." Cal winked, priding himself on the smile he wheedled out of her before he followed after his friend.

## *Chapter Two*

**OWEN** had clearly made a terrible mistake.

He wasn't cut out for the spotlight, high-society hobnobbing, and being catered to like a celebrity just for walking in the front door for a meeting with the mayor. He was a data scientist who was wearing his first of only three good suits amid a closetful of graphic T-shirts and jeans, and his one pair of nice glasses since contacts dried out his eyes, and his other pair was several years old and one prescription behind.

Alyssa had told him to make a list so that every time he realized there was something fundamental he needed, he'd jot it down to get later, since now he could actually afford to do so.

He quickly typed EXTRA PAIR OF GLASSES on his phone below NON-BLUE SUIT COAT and SHOES

THAT AREN'T CONVERSE. How had he missed that all three of his blazers were just different shades of blue? Hopefully no one would notice over the next few days.

He'd purposely not worn a tie because he (1) hated them, (2) owned one and *really* hated that one, and (3) was supposed to be a cool young Silicon Valley type for coming up with these algorithms and so many worthwhile patents at twenty-five. The only "type" he was portraying right now in one of his few plain white T-shirts beneath his blazer was *übernerd*.

"The mayor is expecting you, Mr. Quinn. Right through here." The young woman who'd greeted him gestured to the door at the end of the hallway. "Can I get you anything? Water? Coffee?"

"Oh, uhh… coffee? But with like three sugars and lots of cream till it barely even resembles coffee anymore, if… that's okay?" *Why* was he ever allowed out in public? "Please?"

The woman smiled. "I take it the same way. Only Mayor King is the crazy one who takes it black with no sugar. You'll do fine." With another smile, she moved back down the hallway.

*Wait, the mayor was crazy?* Or was that meant to be an endearment? Owen had only talked to him through proxy until today.

Shoving his phone into his pocket and adjusting the brand-new leather shoulder bag Alyssa and Casey had given him as a going-away present, he knocked on the door before peeking inside.

"Mr. Mayor?"

"Owen! So good to finally meet you in person. Come in."

The mayor stood from his desk and came forward to meet Owen halfway, shaking his hand vigorously. He was young, especially to be running such a large metropolis, but still older than Owen. Definitely a politician with his firm handshake, direct eye contact, and smart suit to compliment his—*wow*, he was attractive.

Which was the last thing Owen should be thinking about his married *boss*. But he was. Tall, well-built, strong jaw.

"Hi!" Owen stammered as he snapped back to attention. "I mean… nice to meet you too, Mr. Mayor. Thank you so much for giving me this opportunity."

"Please, call me Wesley. My staff never takes that to heart, but you're a special case, aren't you, Owen? You're more like *my* boss in this, so let's make sure we do your work proud. Have a seat."

Owen was the boss? He was so in over his head. "Sure! Thank you… uh, Wesley."

"There you go. Drink?" Wesley asked as he returned to his desk.

Owen sat in the seat across from him. "Miss McCabe is getting me coffee."

"Good, good. Now, we're not jumping into anything before we're ready with this new program. While my team has been looking into your recommendations for reorganizing our officers, there are other things to consider."

"Right." Owen forced himself to remain skeptical of where the mayor might go with this. He couldn't be a yes-man. He would not be bullied into letting anyone use his models in a way he didn't approve of, and his shoulder bag was full of suggestions for how to make sure that didn't happen.

"Once things get put into motion," Wesley continued, "there will be a lot of press around this, around you and my office, and the last thing we want is to have it blow up in our faces. As you know, Atlas City has seen a severe increase in criminal activity over the past few years. It's part of why I was elected, because I promised to do something about it. But placing more officers in the neighborhoods most likely to see criminal activity could lead to profiling and general unrest among the citizens.

"My people want to feel safe, Owen, not targeted, so we'll be looking to you to help us prepare our officers appropriately to ensure this is a seamless transition that takes every citizen, especially those living in high-crime areas, into account."

Owen's mind somersaulted as he realized Wesley was telling him exactly what he'd been hoping to hear. He'd prepared so many fumbling speeches for this, but the mayor was already ahead of him.

"Do you understand what I mean, Owen?"

"Yes!" Sitting up straighter after realizing Wesley had been waiting for a response, Owen began pulling research notes from his bag. "Yes, sir. I couldn't agree more. I have several additional preliminary models I'd like to discuss concerning police behavior based on available equipment, like body cameras, group mentality versus single officer or partner deployments, and numerous other things, which should help us prepare your officers to keep everyone accountable." He took a breath to slow down—sometimes he forgot the rest of the world didn't move at his speed. "I want to help people, Mr.… *Wesley*. Not make them fear the police more than they fear criminals."

For a politician, Wesley's smile certainly seemed genuine. "Music to my ears, Owen. You keep us accountable so we can better keep our officers accountable to protect this city—together."

"Thank you," Owen said as the buzzing nerves in his stomach started to shift into excitement. "This is why I chose Atlas City, you know, out of everywhere that vied to pilot this program. Because of you."

"Me? Not because our crime rate's so high?" Wesley grinned.

"Well… that too, but you accepted my proposal without trying to change any of my requirements. I researched the different officials I'd be working with in each city, and you were the only one who seemed like you really cared and wouldn't abuse what I'm trying to do, or look the other way if someone crosses a line. It's good to see that wasn't just fluff for the election. N-not that I assumed—"

Laughter bubbled out of Wesley. "Oh, I like you, Owen. I'm glad you're willing to speak candidly. I want to do this right, so that come next election year, I'll have proven my platform wasn't just *fluff*. So." He slapped his thighs before rising from his desk. "Let's meet my team so they can show you what they've been working on and you can show them your reports. We have a lot of work to do before we get to the major press coverage in a couple weeks. Though of course I have given a few statements to the papers in preparation of your arrival."

"R-right." Owen tried not to trip as he clambered out of his chair.

"Not used to the attention?"

"Not really. I usually prefer hiding *behind* the data." Clutching his papers to his chest, Owen realized he was literally hiding and shoved them into his bag. "At my previous job, I… someone else was always the front man."

*Harrison*. He'd first been interested in Owen's body when they met, then his mind after learning their interests aligned. Harrison was chief technology officer for the software component of Orion Labs, where Owen had also worked—after Harry got him a job. So many of Owen's ideas had helped grow that portion of the company in recent years, and Harrison had taken credit for every single one.

This, finally, was *Owen's*. He wouldn't let his anxieties take that away from him.

"You'll do fine," Wesley said, leading Owen out of the office. "You'll do great. I can already see it."

Everyone kept saying that, which either meant Owen was an obvious ball of stress that people felt sorry for or they honestly had faith in him. Probably both.

"Let's get that coffee from Miss McCabe. You'll need it. It's going to be nonstop from here on out, just to warn you."

"That's okay," Owen said, more relaxed than he'd been the first time he walked down this hallway. "I prefer when things move fast. I've never been good at sitting still."

"Wait till you meet my wife after lunch." Wesley chuckled. "She's the same way."

"Oh, uhh… I have a meeting with the CEO of Nye Industries—"

"*Owen*." Wesley laughed harder. "Didn't anyone tell you? Keri Nye *is* my wife."

Owen had been so focused on researching Wesley's political career, he'd obviously bypassed important personal details—crucial ones. "For real? Wow, you're like a serious power couple."

"So they say—especially her. Ah, here we are." Wesley intercepted Miss McCabe carrying coffees for each of them. With only a glimpse, he easily guessed which one was Owen's. "Thank you, Cynthia. Owen, ready to get to work?"

Owen expected the buzz of nerves and excitement to taper off after that, but it remained constant, especially once he headed to Nye Industries in a car Keri had sent for him and he got to meet the First Lady of Atlas City in person.

"Owen! We are going to impress the *pants* off you today." The woman shook his hand almost more fervently than her husband had. They were like Business Barbie and Ken, Owen noted—she was stunning. "Not literally of course." She winked. "Crap, did I just give a first impression of sexual harassment? Coz we can start over."

Owen could only answer with flustered laughter, but she barely paused before moving on. The flurry of Keri Nye and the speed with which she was in total control after tripping over her words was what Owen aspired to be like someday. He never had any illusions about recovering from foot-in-mouth syndrome completely, but she wasn't even ruffled.

"Let's see if you consider us up to snuff to steal some of your time from the mayor's office."

"Is that really okay?" Owen shuffled after her into the large skyscraper that humbled the mayor's office with its modern design.

"Conflict of interest with the mayor, you mean? Not to worry. I didn't call in any favors with my husband. You agreed to meet with me all on your own, remember?"

"Right! No, I know, but he won't be upset if I split my time? There's so much to do…."

"This is your show, Owen," she said, leading him briskly to the elevator for his tour of the building like she was just another office worker instead of president and CEO. "You decide what you want. You're only contracted as part-time at the mayor's office, specifically because you wanted time for other opportunities. Well, that's what I'm here for."

Owen huffed like he'd been running a marathon when the elevator door closed behind them, bringing them up to the 32nd floor. "I'm just not used to having…."

"Options?"

*Freedom.* "Yeah."

"This is your moment." Keri nudged his shoulder, betraying her youth and easygoing nature, which was part of what Owen had liked about Wesley too. Anyone too uptight to be at ease with their peers—and those technically below them—could never understand the common man. "We're trying to please *you* today. Enjoy it."

The final reason Owen had chosen Atlas City was because of Nye Industries and Walker Tech. Both were local and thriving software companies that did so much more than create marketing platforms or cloud technology. Walker Tech was working on nanomachines to better distribute gene therapy to terminally ill patients, and Nye Industries had developed a prototype for an electromagnet-pulsing chip that could help thousands of people with debilitating spinal injuries. If Owen's predictive models could in any way help these companies with their next projects, he wanted to be a part of that.

"I hope Keri hasn't scared you off yet," Frank Holtz said after Owen's tour of the R&D labs.

Keri had been called away to an investor meeting, handing Owen over to Frank for the duration of his tour. As head of Design Innovation, Frank had been the lead engineer in coming up with the biostimulator chip for paralysis patients, so Owen was keen to hear his perspective on the company's direction.

Owen also got the impression that Keri had a soft spot for people with her same rambling tendencies—which Frank had in spades. Owen could admit that it eased him to be around someone who stumbled into unfortunate ways of wording things even more than he did.

"You're gay, right?" Frank blurted as they were passing a cluster of people at a water cooler. Owen nearly tripped over his own feet. "*That* was inappropriate. It's just that… I'm gay too. At least my husband thinks so." He elbowed Owen with a laugh, then clammed up again when Owen wasn't sure how to respond. "Bad joke again. Sorry. I just mean… I'd heard you were gay, and you know how we tend to move in packs, so if you felt concerned for any reason being in a new city, Keri and the mayor are, like, super cool besides being genuine and extremely attractive people. Not that I think about the mayor's attractiveness!"

Owen had to laugh. The awkwardness had reached a boiling point, but for once, he wasn't the cause.

"You're running straight for Walker Tech and never looking back, aren't you?" Frank said.

"No! No. I mean, I'd like to work with both companies. And also, yes… I'm gay. Just nothing more to say at the moment."

"Bad breakup?"

Once again, Owen faltered. If Frank knew he was gay, that meant he knew about Harrison. Orion Labs in Middleton was well-known, even if the small software side of things wasn't as big a player as anything here. The right circles likely knew about Owen's ex without him having to say a word.

"Which you obviously don't want to talk about." Frank broke into another harried ramble. "But if you ever need some friendly faces around for a game night or drink at the bar, my husband and I have *incredibly* friendly faces. Him more so, coz obviously I think he's perfect. That's why I married him. He's also a much better conversationalist, I promise."

As uncomfortable as things turning toward Harrison had made Owen feel, he wasn't upset with Frank. "I appreciate that, but I'm still settling in right now. In fact, when I get home, hopefully I'll actually have furniture."

"Is that why you had that catalog in your bag? Not that I was snooping." Frank raised his hands to defend himself. "I just… noticed."

"Yeah. In case I didn't hear from them, but they texted me awhile ago that they—" And just then, when Owen decided to take the catalog out of his bag, the business card that should have been tucked securely into its designated page fluttered out like making a jailbreak, and Frank bent to retrieve it.

"I got it."

"Wait—"

"Nick of Time Escort Service?"

*Shit.*

"Hey, I know this place!" Frank smiled, then blanched when he saw Owen's expression. "Not like *that*. I mean, maybe once or twice like that, before me and my husband, obviously, I don't, I'm… not judging, is what I mean." He thrust the card back at Owen.

*Wonderful.* At least there wasn't anyone near them in the hallway right now. Owen needed to remember to blame Alyssa if he ended up with a "reputation" at work. "It's for dates only, if I needed one for events or anything. Not that I think I'll use it. Probably never. I just don't really want to date for real right now, you know?"

"I get it," Frank said, genuinely seeming to understand. "Plus, I'm sort of glad that fell out."

"Really?"

"Now when you look back on your first day at Nye Industries, hopefully you'll remember your totally unwarranted embarrassment over my completely justified humiliation."

Owen laughed. Frank and Keri made him feel like he could belong here as an escape from the more daunting task of managing the mayor's program. If what he'd experienced the past few hours was an indication of the next several weeks, months, and hopefully more to come, he might actually be able to do this.

**CAL** entered his apartment with a crick in his neck but a satisfied sensation buzzing through him. Piper did tend to twist him into interesting positions, but as always, it had been a worthwhile and lucrative evening.

Now that it was late and Cal had the opportunity to relax, he looked forward to a long shower and nothing to disturb him until morning. He was a night owl by nature, since his hours of operation tended to go late and he usually had the freedom to sleep in.

Relieving himself of his jacket and heading to his sound system, he turned on his mix of classical crooners. Nothing relaxed him like Ella Fitzgerald or Tony Bennett.

Tony's version of "Cold Cold Heart" began to play, and Cal closed his eyes to ease into his private space and personal thoughts. His home was his and his alone, a place untouched by anything he did outside these walls. Only Rhys and Lara had been inside, and his sister, who rarely visited. More often he visited her in Middleton, because this space was his—his escape.

A frown passed over his features as the old thread of peace didn't fill him like it used to. Lately his quiet home felt more suffocating than he cared to admit, and he couldn't understand why. Midlife crisis, his sister had teased him after he turned forty. Maybe. And if so, how dull. How ordinary and expected. Just because he was getting older didn't mean he had to have some secret desire to settle down. It didn't mean he was lonely for something his clients couldn't offer. He was perfectly content.

But content was something he strived for knowing happiness was rare. Happiness was still nice, but experiencing it was happening less and less often. Maybe that's why Cal felt off around Merlin, and the man himself had nothing to hide. He couldn't be sure now, and it bothered him that the peace he craved was being chased away by errant paranoia.

He took his shower anyway, long and hot, as he hummed to the music playing over the speakers wired through his apartment. It was a studio, but a large one, in whites and gray and navy blue, with only a few closets and the bathroom separate, while his bedroom merely had a wall that blocked the view to the bed from the entryway. He didn't need excess privacy when he lived alone.

Running a hand over the short buzz of his hair once he'd toweled off and wrapped himself in his softest robe, Cal sat at his desk near the window to peruse his calendar. As expected, Lara had emailed him an updated copy of his schedule.

A new request had also come through from Merlin, since the system took too long, and he was still on the roster until the paperwork finished. Cal wouldn't respond. Even if he was overreacting, he was done with the man, and good riddance. His other regulars were enough.

He checked his finances, then his calendar outside of work, which included upper-class events to avoid where he might run into clients, past or present. His sister and very few close friends called him meticulous to his face and anal behind his back—*and* to his face, if that friend was Rhys.

Cal didn't mind. It comforted him to have control down to the minute detail. There were probably psychology papers written about how neglected children with abusive parents sought out destructive ways of controlling their lives—textbook really. Cal wasn't a slave to predictability or fate, but he wouldn't pretend that having a mother who'd left and a father he would have been better off without hadn't led to some of his life choices.

Still, what he wanted now was something to stir up the monotony that left him feeling like something was missing from his life, something he couldn't put a name to.

After glancing at the clock to ensure it wasn't too late, he dialed his sister's number.

"Missing my sweet voice, Cal?"

"Always, sis." He leaned back in his chair to peer out the window. It wasn't the most spectacular view in town, but it was lovely all the same. Maybe he'd just needed Claire's voice in his ear instead of Tony Bennett. "How are the kids?"

"Good batch this year. Just starting beginners figure skating."

"Your favorite."

"When's the last time *you* put on a pair of skates?"

"Lord knows." Cal chuckled. "Sibling activity next time I'm in town?"

"You're on." Claire ran the youth programs at Middleton Community Center. She hadn't "settled down" either, no husband or kids of her own, but she was a good decade younger than Cal. "How are *you*, Calvin? Any princes added to your clients yet?" She always asked that, wondering when he'd be whisked away to a life of luxury by some benevolent benefactor, but real life wasn't like *Pretty Woman*.

"Princess, in a way, but I dubbed her 'Prince' in the books just for you."

"Really? Like, a real princess? From where?"

"Now, sis, you know I can't divulge specifics."

"Spoilsport." He could hear her pout over the phone, but it was enough of a concession that he'd mentioned Prince since he'd been seeing her for a while now. "What can I say, your glamorous lifestyle does sound appealing on occasion."

"You love your life," he said, which was all he'd ever wanted for her.

"I do. Do you?"

"Of course, why wouldn't I?"

"You have that tone again...."

"What tone?" Cal frowned at how well she read him even over the phone.

"*Wistful.* Like you're up in your head too much. I just want you to be happy."

"I'm not... unhappy." Wincing at not being able to uphold the lie he'd had ready, Cal fumbled to continue, "I have full control over my life."

"Yeah? Well sometimes *losing* control is needed to shake things up. Don't be opposed to unexpected surprises."

"What are you now, my horoscope?"

"Just your concerned sister, smartass. I hate that you're all alone so far away."

Shrugging off the tension in his shoulders, Cal pushed from his chair to walk closer to the window, staring over the skyscrapers that were very different from the ones he'd grown up with. He'd moved here to put some distance between him and his father years ago, but Claire wasn't the only thing he missed.

"I'll visit soon. And I'm not alone. I have Rhys."

"And when's the last time you two had a deep conversation?"

"I have Lara for that."

"Who you almost dated."

"We didn't almost date," Cal defended. "I stole a kiss under the mistletoe in her office last Christmas. Rule number two: never date a coworker."

"What's rule number one?" Claire asked.

Glancing down at the open calendar on his computer, Cal fought a sneer he couldn't wrap his head around. "Never date a client. I'll catch up with you later, okay?"

"Okay, Cal, but like I said, change could be good for you. We'll talk soon."

*Change.* Cal could use some change, but toward what, he had no idea.


**OWEN'S** first week had gone wonderfully. It really had. Everyone was great, and he did intend to take Frank up on that offer to reclaim his status as a third wheel for a married couple some night soon. But he was exhausted, and whenever he got home after a long day, he wished he had someone to talk to who wasn't a coworker or hundreds of miles away.

As he hung up his jacket and looked around his newly furnished apartment, he considered the weekend ahead with no plans whatsoever to look forward to... and wondered what Harrison might be up to.

His phone ringing interrupted him.

"Hello?"

"Don't call him," his best friend's voice came over the line.

"Mario? How did you know?" Owen said, plopping down onto the sofa. It was a large, plush, half-square shape in deep burgundy that easily could have allowed a grown man to stretch out on either side. Owen lay that way now, staring at the empty side opposite him.

"I know you, dude," Mario said, one of the few college friends Owen had connected with, and someone who'd known him *before* he met Harrison. "You're hundreds of miles away from your friends, and you don't make new ones easy. You're probably sitting at home alone, pining after that asshole because you're lonely."

"Why are you always right?" Owen groaned. Everything else was perfect, and Harrison still managed to ruin his evening.

"Do me a favor, man, okay? Go out. Meet someone new. Meet anyone new. Don't give in and call him. It's been months. You're finally over the hurdle. And remember, you left him for a reason. You deserve something so much better."

If it hadn't been for Alyssa, Casey, and Mario, Owen probably would have gone back to Harrison out of sheer fear after the first few days. "I just wish I could skip the hard part of meeting someone, ya know, get right to... having someone over for dinner, someone who'd talk with me, hold me, and not only want me for sex." There he went again, sounding like a Lifetime Channel movie, but it was the truth.

Mario hadn't once belittled him for it. "I get it, man. Too bad you can't hire someone for that sorta thing."

Glancing at his shoulder bag on the floor, which still had the catalog in it because Owen had been debating ordering more pieces all week, the last thing that sprang to mind was the furniture in its pages. "Yeah...."

"Dude, I'm kidding!"

"Me too!" Owen sprang up and turned to face the coffee table. "That would be... totally weird."

"I'm serious, O," Mario said. "Go out. Have fun. Trust yourself. I wanna come visit sometime, but only after you've settled in and can actually show me around."

Alyssa had said something similar earlier in the week. "That sounds awesome."

"Be good, man, okay? You're gonna kick ass at everything coming your way. I know it."

"Thanks, Mario. And I'll take your advice. I promise."

He wanted to. After all, Mario knew him almost as well as Alyssa did. They'd bonded after having various classes together, and Mario had gone on to become an engineer. There were many things they could talk shop about, or just wax on for hours about comic books and sci-fi movies. But Mario's biggest appeal as a friend was how sometimes he just knew when Owen was about to do something profoundly stupid and stepped in to intervene, like a sixth sense.

Tapping his fingers on his shiny new coffee table, Owen tried to dismiss how antsy he felt on his first Friday night in the city. He wasn't the partying type. He didn't want to go out to a bar or a club or anything like that. He wanted a date without having to find one, and not a one-night stand either. He didn't want sex. All Harrison had ever wanted from him was to *take, take, take*. Owen wanted company without the hang-ups.

He snatched his bag from the floor before he could second-guess himself and took out the catalog. He'd left the business card inside all week when he easily could have thrown it away. Pulling out his laptop next, he went to the web address listed on the card, something else he hadn't dared to do all week.

It was a fairly classy layout, all things considered, and Alyssa was right that everything was worded in a "don't expect sex, but it's totally on the table" sort of way for legal reasons. But the rules would be his to set; he could have whatever he wanted, no "sexy times" required. He could even choose the type of man he wanted, sort of the same way he'd picked out his furniture—which was a terrible thing to think about a person, yet there he was, looking at a *catalog* of attractive men.

They listed things like height, age, ethnicity, likes and dislikes, even talents. Owen told himself he was not hung up on Harrison just because he filtered the selection to men over forty.

There was even a note at the top of the page listing a bonus cost for "anything goes," and wow was it steep, but considering that what Owen wanted was far from the norm, for someone to hold him skin against skin without anything more sordid taking place, maybe he fell under that category. He had the money, and he needed something he could control just this once.

Dialing the number, he felt his heart in his throat but refused to chicken out.

"Nick of Time Escort Service. How may I help you?"

## *Chapter Three*

**DICK** would have been proud. Cal was taking on a new client. At least for the night. He doubted it would turn into anything ongoing, but when the request came through, he hadn't been able to deny his curiosity and agreed to one evening's work.

"Owen Quinn? The one the mayor's been talking about who's going to turn the city's criminal activity on its head?"

"That's the one," Lara had said over the phone. She always called if a request was pressing and from someone not currently on the agency's roster.

"He check out?"

"Squeaky clean. Medical records from only a couple weeks ago, probably for the move. Maybe even ordered by the mayor. Or maybe he wanted a fresh start from Middleton. That's where you're from, isn't it?"

"Don't change the subject. What else does his profile say?"

"I forwarded you the request. Have a look. He wants you for tonight, as soon as possible. I know you don't do last minute, but I figured it might give you a laugh. He didn't even select backups."

Cal sat at his computer and pulled up the email, which included a link to the request form. It listed similar items to what the escorts put on their profiles, along with the medical report and a photo—which caused Cal to snort.

"*That's* the picture he sent?"

Lara could barely contain her snickering. "He didn't have a recent photo, so he took a selfie."

It wasn't terrible, but the image was too close to be flattering. Cal could mostly only make out a dopey smile, black-framed glasses, and a floof of brunet hair. Owen looked even younger than his profile suggested.

Owen Quinn was a twenty-five-year-old data scientist from Middleton, about Cal's height, with a clean bill of health. Likes included lounge music and show tunes, sci-fi movies, and quiet evenings in—right up Cal's alley—while dislikes only stated clubbing and crowds.

Then came the note at the bottom—*anything goes*. Bit of a misnomer, since escorts always had the prerogative to say no, but with the extra fee involved, it was a rare occurrence that what was requested was so outlandish they'd refuse. Usually it fell more under embarrassing for the client to voice aloud than dangerous or depraved. Still, Cal was intrigued.

"Tell him yes. I'll be there in thirty minutes."

"Seriously?"

The profile was so innocuous for someone to request "anything goes," and that photo, while ridiculous, made him wonder what the real thing might look like. Besides, Cal had an empty slot to fill, and his instincts were rarely wrong.

"One of three things will happen when I arrive," he said, leaning back in his chair to stare at the profile. "One, he'll prove to be an insufferable, entitled brat, who made it rich young and wants to splurge his first Friday night in the city. Two, this is all an elaborate prank by some of his friends, and he'll have no idea why I'm showing up at his door. Or three… he'll surprise me.

"If it's the first option, I reserve the right to leave if he can't be dealt with, if it's the second, I'll hardly be fazed and be on my way, but if it's the third—" He grinned as a flutter of excitement stirred in his belly. "—who knows what the evening might bring."

"Ever the gambling man, Calvin?" Lara said.

"Thirty minutes," he repeated and hung up as soon as she acknowledged him.

Those thirty minutes were gone now, with two to spare as Cal headed up the elevator in one of the nicest high-rise apartment buildings in Atlas City. It was possible he'd gone overboard with his attire for the evening, but regardless of how things turned out, he wanted to make Owen's jaw drop when he opened the door.

Cal had chosen his nicest three-piece suit in blue, white shirt, navy-and-silver paisley tie, vest double-breasted but jacket single, with a heather-gray wool coat and checkered blue-and-gray scarf to complement the ensemble. He even had the tease of a red handkerchief in his top jacket pocket for color.

Right on time, Cal approached the penthouse apartment door and knocked twice. He heard the sound of scrambling feet on the other side, but instead of a lurch of the door opening, there was a pause, like the occupant was second-guessing himself before he slowly opened the door.

Cal's first sight of Owen Quinn was already a pleasant surprise. The selfie hadn't done him justice, because there were dimples in that pale skin and sparking hazel eyes behind the glasses. He wore his hair stylishly enough, but he was less successful in the fashion department, given the button-up sweater over his collared shirt. It matched fine, blocked off in four distinct colors of gray, red, burgundy, and black, but it wouldn't be gracing any magazine covers. The skinny jeans fit well, though, and he was— hmm—only wearing socks.

"H-hi!" Owen stammered with a quick blush spreading over his cheeks in rosy scarlet. Not an insufferable, entitled brat, then. "You're from the… I-I mean, y-you're the…." He paused for breath. "Calvin, right?"

"Cal," Cal corrected, though a few contacts insisted on using his full name. "Cal Mercer. And you're Owen Quinn." It wasn't a question anymore; this was definitely Cal's "evenings in, sci-fi loving" client for the night.

"That's me," Owen said, scratching the back of his head like he never spent even a moment out of motion. Cal would have pegged him for a virgin being this jumpy if he hadn't put "a few months ago" for his last sexual activity.

Owen was preoccupied enough with taking in Cal's appearance that he didn't say anything else right away or step aside to let him in. The jaw-dropping portion of the evening was a resounding success.

"Well, Owen, seeing as how you aren't wearing shoes, I assume we're not going out, so… shall I come in?"

"Oh! Of course!" Now, finally, Owen made room for Cal to move past him into the apartment. "And no, we're not going out. I'd rather stay in, if that's okay?"

*If that's okay.* "I think you misunderstand how this works." Cal refrained from betraying his own jaw-drop when he got a look at the apartment, with windows all along one wall that put his own view of Atlas City to shame and an eclectic but personable taste level in decorating that he found instantly charming. The space had to be twice the square feet of his own apartment. "*Whatever you want* is okay. You set the stage, and I perform to your specifications. Sound fun?" Finishing a cursory survey of the apartment, Cal snapped his attention back to Owen.

"Y-yeah," he exhaled as he closed the door. "Sorry, I know I seem like a nervous wreck, I'm just out of practice with… human interaction, apparently." He laughed at himself and scratched the back of his head again, before jerking forward like he'd forgotten something important. "Let me take your coat."

"Thank you," Cal said, allowing Owen to relieve him of his jacket, scarf included, and hang it on a coatrack by the door. Adorable *and* polite. Cal was won over by his decision to come here more every minute. "And you can relax. There's nothing to be nervous about. It's my job to make you feel at ease. Now, what will we be up to this evening if we're… staying in?" He gave Owen his most seductive glance, a flick of his eyes downward and back up to Owen's face with a crook to his smile.

Owen almost tripped over the bottom half of the coatrack, and Cal had to wonder how far down that slender neck the scarlet went. "I-I kinda wanted to start with dinner?" he squeaked, then cleared his throat and made a hasty retreat toward the kitchen.

The skinny jeans fit *very* well.

"I finally stocked up on groceries and was craving something home-cooked," he said while Cal followed him to the long island that separated the kitchen from the rest of the apartment. "Since the week was so busy, and I kept eating on the go. I'm not good at too many dishes, but this one of my mom's is perfect. If you haven't eaten yet?" He looked back at Cal with sudden worry.

Cal had eaten. He always ate a little before seeing a client, as he never knew whether a meal would be included, but he'd kept to a light snack just in case. "I can eat. Smells lovely." It did. Tomato based, maybe a little cheesy, spicy.

Creasing his dimples further with his smile, Owen gave the pan on the stove a stir and turned off the burners. He had plates ready with salad portioned out, waiting to be joined by the main course. Behind Cal, to the left of the entryway, was a quaint dining table with different colored chairs. Two glasses and a bottle of wine waited for them as well.

"It's this goulash, casserole thing," Owen said as he dished up a helping for both of them. "Goes really well with wine, and I got a few bottles as going-away presents, and some welcome gifts from Nye Industries and…." His brow creased as he walked toward the table, carrying both plates. "I think this one is from Walker Tech? I haven't found the time to meet with their CEO yet. It's been crazy. Oh." He spun toward Cal after setting the table. "I'm—"

"I know who you are, Owen. I read the papers." Cal took a seat in the blue chair, leaving Owen to sit at his left in the red. "Must be exciting."

"It is!" Owen started to pour them each a glass of the no-doubt highly expensive pinot noir. "Terrifying, but exciting. Everyone's made me feel really at home so far."

"Yet you're spending your Friday night alone?" Cal had never been good at holding back his inquisitiveness. It's what kept him one step ahead of other people.

"I wanted something low-key. Quiet." Owen closed his eyes and breathed in as if to better hear the music playing that Cal had almost missed—*Sinatra*. So far, Owen hadn't told any lies on his profile, and his lashes fluttered prettily against his cheeks when he opened his eyes. "Sorry, I'm trying to relax. I'm just bad with change, and there's been *a lot* of change in my life the past few months."

"More than moving?" Cal asked, thinking it rather serendipitous that Owen was looking for balance while Cal was looking to shake things up, yet both might find what they wanted in the same place.

A shadow darkened Owen's expression. "Yeah...," he said quietly—a nerve to be avoided, it seemed.

Cal would have to pay closer attention. Not that he'd never had someone call upon his services to help them get over something difficult—divorce, being fired, hitting a milestone birthday while still single. Everyone had their hang-ups and reasons for wanting an escort instead of a blind date, but Owen remained an enigma as far as what he wanted and what "anything goes" might mean.

Taking his first bite of the meal in front of him, Cal couldn't wait to find out more.

**THIS** is delicious," Cal said, surprise in his eyes that made Owen think he meant it instead of just being kind. It was tough to know how to read the man since he might be especially proficient with acting to always give a client what they wanted. Maybe Owen couldn't trust anything he said or how he reacted, but he had a feeling Cal wasn't the type to ever do something he didn't want.

He was also far hotter in person than any pictures portrayed. Early forties, even with a dusting of gray in his closely cropped hair, but his face made him look five if not ten years younger. His features were flawlessly carved, blue eyes hypnotic next to tan skin. And the *suit*—it was like having dinner with a movie star.

Sure, Cal's photos on the agency's website had been similar, showing him off in smart outfits and strong poses, but to have chosen him in a catalog one moment and have him here now barely an hour later was surreal. There hadn't been any contest among the other escorts in Cal's age range once Owen found his profile. For one, they had similar interests, and Cal didn't look anything like Harrison. He looked like the sort of prince charming fantasy man Owen would have dreamed up as a teenager.

"Th-thanks," he stammered again, struggling to remind himself that there was no pressure tonight. He didn't have to impress Cal, and nothing would happen that he didn't want. "It was always my favorite dish my mom used to make."

"She doesn't make it anymore?"

Owen coughed on his first bite and took a sip of wine to clear his throat. "Uhh… no." Why did he have to walk into *that* conversation within the first five minutes? He stared down at his plate. "After my parents… passed away, it was the only meal I could remember well enough to replicate. It took me years to get it right. My adopted dad and sister were really supportive guinea pigs, though." He glanced up with a shy smile.

If Cal was bothered to learn Owen was an orphan, he didn't show it. "I'm sorry, I keep mentioning things that upset you."

"No, it's fine." Owen twirled his fork for another bite. "My parents have been on my brain a lot lately because of the job. I came up with the models to better predict criminal activity because of how they died. Robbery gone wrong. I was ten, almost eleven. I was playing in the backyard when it happened. Didn't even notice anything was wrong until I got hungry and went inside for dinner.

"The thing is, there had been a rash of break-ins near our neighborhood. If someone had been paying closer attention to the data, they might have had more officers around, which could have dissuaded the thieves and…. Well—" Owen bowed his head again, self-conscious of how intense he could get on the subject. "—there's no way to know, but I like to think that what I'm doing now might prevent what happened to me from happening to someone else."

"That's very noble," Cal said, smiling with an authenticity that was separate from his more seductive glances, which made Owen even tinglier when their eyes met.

"Feels selfish sometimes."

"You're allowed to be selfish. Opportunities at Nye Industries and Walker Tech must be… profitable." Cal raised the glass of wine before taking a drink.

"They do amazing things. I'm hoping to contract work with both companies. But they compete in certain areas, so it could get tricky. It'll have to be noncompeting departments, and I'll have to be really careful about information I share. Assuming neither side tries to make me sign some crazy nondisclosure or says they won't let me work with the other. I don't think they're like that, though, since they partner for charity work sometimes." Owen took another bite, another swig of wine, telling himself to stop being so chatty. He tended to ramble when he was nervous—or all the time really. "What about you?" he asked.

"What about me?" Cal recaptured his smirk.

"Your profile told me basic things, but what didn't it say? Or is that inappropriate?" Owen had no idea what the precedent was being with an escort. "Am I not supposed to ask anything personal?"

The good humor in Cal's eyes kept Owen's nerves from ramping up again. "What do you want to know?"

"Family?"

"Mostly just me and my sister. She's in Middleton."

"Mine too." Owen sat forward as he grabbed at the familiar thread. "My sister and her husband run this bar in Uptown, *Impulse*. Alyssa loves knowing everyone's secrets and being able to give advice, you know like that bartender who always has the answers to life's questions? I say she just likes to gossip." He chuckled.

"I'll have to see if my sister's ever been there," Cal said. "Claire works at the community center with the youth programs."

"That's cool." And so normal, not that Owen had a right to make assumptions just because Cal was an escort. "It's obvious why I came to Atlas City. What about you?"

"Needed a change." Cal shrugged. "Been here for years now."

"Maybe you can give me some pointers."

"Like where to find a good tailor?"

Owen laughed. Cal must have noticed how much he'd been staring at his suit. "Please. I need to get some work clothes for next week before they realize I only have three blazers that are practically identical. My wardrobe's a disaster."

"I got that impression." Cal nodded at Owen's sweater.

"Is this not good?" He'd spent more time picking out what to wear than cooking. Though compared to Cal, he did look drab. "Shoot, I really like this sweater…."

"It's fine. Maybe more suited for a man a decade or two older than *me*."

Another laugh escaped Owen's lips. Cal's teasing soothed him rather than coming across as mean-spirited. "No wonder Alyssa calls it my Mr. Rogers sweater." After undoing the buttons, he shrugged it off and laid it over the back of his chair, leaving behind his simple black button-down.

"Much better," Cal said. "Maybe if you decide you'd like to see me again, I can take you shopping."

"Really?" Owen felt his face heat up at the thought. "That would be amazing."

"For now, I can give you some recommendations. You'd look nice in something more—" He did that eye-glance down Owen's body that made him feel as if steam was pouring from his ears like a cartoon character. "—*fitted*."

Hastily shoving another bite of goulash into his mouth, Owen tried to avoid how terrible he was at taking compliments. Harrison had only praised him when he wanted something.

The faint music in the background changed to Ella Fitzgerald singing "Someone to Watch Over Me," one of Owen's mother's favorites, and he watched Cal close his eyes with the pleasure of listening.

"Your taste in music makes up for the sweater," he said, all charm through his mild ribbing. "Part of what convinced me to accept you tonight."

"Yeah? I, uhh… left something out of my profile about that."

"Oh?" Cal raised an eyebrow at him.

"I also like metal."

The shock of laughter that left Cal sounded entirely sincere. "Show tunes and jazz from Mom, metal from Dad, I take it?"

"Actually, Mom was the Megadeth fan." The more they laughed and talked openly, the more Owen felt at ease, even discussing his parents, which was a rare occurrence. "I listen to metal when I work, Ella for relaxing."

"Fair enough. I won't consider it a deal breaker." Cal even pulled a fork from between his lips and drank his wine with allure.

Owen was enamored by everything about him. Even if Cal was only a fantasy, he was still tangible. "Your likes and dislikes were definitely what won me over about you. I mean, also because you're *gorgeous*. Uhh...." And then he had to go and put his foot in his mouth again. Owen drank more wine to hide how mortified he was to have said that. He should probably slow down considering what a lightweight he was.

Cal was just easy to talk to, even though Owen got flustered whenever the man's eyes penetrated too deeply or he said something flirtatious. He was *supposed* to be flirting, showing interest, making Owen feel wanted. It's what he was paid to do. But even if it was all an act, Owen felt a genuineness in Cal's smiles.

"You decorate this place yourself?" he asked.

"Yep. I need some rugs and artwork I think." Owen turned to take in what he'd done so far. He still wasn't pulling off the hip young tech genius he was supposed to be, but he didn't care. He wasn't a modern or art deco type guy; he preferred plush furniture in bright colors. "Debating what to get next is a nice distraction from being alone. Wow." He cringed after saying that. "I am super depressing, aren't I?"

"Not at all," Cal said. "You're new in town, just getting your feet. Not everyone is the easily sociable type. But I have to ask."

"Yeah?" He whirled to face Cal, wondering if now would be when the man asked what came *after* dinner, which Owen was sure he'd make a fool of himself explaining.

"You said sci-fi movie fan. What's your favorite?"

"Oh!" Owen brightened. "I don't know. Wow. I can only choose one? I guess I have a soft spot for *The Fifth Element*. Though *Terminator 2* was the first movie that ever made me cry."

"*Terminator 2* made you cry?"

"At the end, you know, when Arnie's being lowered into the molten metal and he does the thumbs-up thing—cried like a baby." Owen was way past being embarrassed by that. "I also have deep love for *The Thing* and *Forbidden Planet*."

"Leslie Nielsen *Forbidden Planet*?" Cal's interest couldn't possibly be fake with the way his features smoothed out.

"It totally holds up, don't you think? Oh, but I hate *Blade Runner*."

"Well now," Cal said as if scandalized, "I was all on board until that. I don't think we can be friends anymore."

How did this man keep making Owen laugh so easily? "It's so overrated. And *boring*. Visually gorgeous, I get it, and the message is great about 'what does it mean to be human,' but the storytelling does not work for me."

"So it should have had the voiceover?"

"God no. Have you heard some of it? It's so much worse!"

"That I will give you." Cal shared Owen's mirth with a sideways twitch to his smile. "But in general, we'll have to agree to disagree."

Mario said the same thing. He worshipped *Blade Runner*.

It surprised Owen how quickly they ate during the conversation. And went through the wine—*wow*. Refilling both glasses, while he didn't want to overeat, he felt like he could use the extra liquid courage, especially when Cal took a slow sip and then left his wine on the table as he stood.

Sammy Davis Jr.'s "Something's Gotta Give" taunted Owen over the sound system. His breath caught, leaving him frozen in place when the wineglass was taken from him and Cal curled his fingers around the back of his chair to lean in close.

"Dinner was lovely, Owen, but you paid for anything goes," he said, low and lilting. "Now, I maintain the option to refuse anything I'm not up for, but I'm curious. Just what do you want from me to pay so much for a night?"

A shiver rippled through Owen, but it was pleasant, not something to make him lean away, he just didn't know where else to move. "It's nothing weird. I hope it's not weird…." He'd always been the weird kid. Orphan, nerd, *gay*, too skinny, too much of a doormat.

"Tell me," Cal urged Owen with a sultry whisper. "What would you like me to do? Shall we move into the bedroom?" He cast his gaze to the open doorway at the far side of the main room. Owen had a real bed in there now. Simple, no headboard, with slate gray sheets. It was everything else in the room that was colorful, like the books on his shelves and the stained-glass lamp on the nightstand.

"Y-yes," he said and accepted the hand Cal offered.

The strength in the other man made Owen giddy as he was pulled from the chair. He was being led by the hand into his bedroom by the most attractive man he'd ever seen up close and whose voice made him tremble down to his toes.

"Whatever shall we do once we get in there?"

"It's n-not... I-I just...." Owen was a stuttering, stumbling mess, a complete goon trying to find the words to explain.

"Relax, remember?" Cal brought Owen's fingers to his lips and kissed them just as their feet crossed the threshold. He was gentle for all his strength, tugging Owen forward and turning them so he could coax Owen to sit on the bed. Backing up a step, he traced long fingers down the length of his tie. "Would you like me to undress for you?"

"*Yes*," Owen said, maybe too eagerly, but he'd decided before Cal arrived that he wanted skin contact. "Just not *everything*," he added when Cal started to loosen his tie. "Keep your underwear on. Please."

"You're assuming I'm wearing any." Cal winked.

"You're *not*?"

"Only teasing," Cal rumbled with laughter. "We can start there."

The paisley tie came undone in two sure jerks on the knot. Coiling it around his hand, Cal slid his jacket off and set both items on the chair beside Owen's bed, where he also toed off his shoes. Then he started to undo his vest.

"I-I want...."

"Yes, Owen?" Cal's voice saying Owen's name like that was making this harder—*much* harder.

"I don't want you to do anything unless I ask you to," Owen said in a rush.

Cal paused as his vest fluttered open, picking up on the seriousness of the request. "Of course. Anything you want. *Only* what you want." His fingers undid the buttons on his shirt like a weaver pulling thread. The crisp white stood out starkly against his skin, and the shade of blue in the vest and slacks complimented him like he'd been created with that color in mind.

Watching the slow, precise movements of Cal taking off his clothes, Owen brought up a quaking hand to his own shirt. He had to undress himself. He'd never make it through this if Cal offered to help.

"It's okay," Cal said, the calm, even tone of his voice reminding Owen that it *was*, that he didn't need to shake or be afraid, even though no one had touched him since….

*No*, he didn't want to think about Harrison.

"Your speed, Owen. Your rules." Cal opened his shirt like parting the curtain to a great prize and shrugged it from his shoulders to fall to the floor.

He wasn't the broadest of men, but if his features were carved from marble, then his body was just as impeccable, especially the touches of softness around his muscle tone and the diamond of chest hair that thinned into a line on its way down until it disappeared into his underwear. No waxed six-pack—this was better. There was even the hint of a scar along Cal's collarbone to remind Owen that he wasn't some statue come to life, he was real.

"Your *everything*," Cal said.

Owen nodded, feeling empowered by his belief in Cal. The usual bashfulness over being too skinny didn't surface as he removed his shirt. He started to undo his jeans just as Cal unbuttoned his slacks, and he had to wonder when he'd last seen another man in an intimate setting who wasn't *Harry*.

Seeking to banish any remaining traces of his ex, Owen kicked his jeans to the floor, impatient now for Cal to join him. As soon as the other man was left in only snug boxer briefs, Owen scooted up the mattress.

"On the bed. Under the covers with me." He wasn't usually good at giving orders, but the way Cal listened to him, grinned and slinked after him from the foot of the bed, made it easy to stay confident. Cal didn't touch him when Owen yanked down the covers and they slid beneath together, not until Owen reached for him first.

Taking hold of Cal's arms, Owen turned onto his side and wrapped Cal around him like a blanket, snuggling back against his chest and feeling instant relief in the contact of skin. "*Yes*... like this," he said as if he'd been holding his breath for months.

He could feel that Cal was hard, stiffening behind him against his hip. Of course he was; Owen was too, and he hadn't explained that he didn't want to go further. Part of him wondered if he should change his mind. He could, he knew. Cal expected him to ask for more, but this... this was all Owen wanted despite the stirrings in his body. Cal's warmth and kindness and comfort— things Harrison had only pretended to give him.

It felt better than Owen expected, and he clung tightly to the arms around his waist, choked by the emotions catching in his throat as he basked in having someone with him who wouldn't ask for more than he could give.

**THERE** were plenty of attractive men in the agency's catalog closer to Owen's age, even a few Cal respected for their tastes aligning closely with his own, enough that Owen could have found someone younger with ease. He wondered if the decision to have *him* tonight was purely aesthetic or a conscious choice on Owen's part to have an older man, but Cal had pried enough with questions during dinner.

Owen was such a fragile, sweet kid, blushing and endearing through it all, making Cal want to please him all the more and give him everything he asked for.

"You smell even better than I thought you would." Owen sighed in pure bliss—just what Cal had hoped to instill in him.

Owen felt amazing pressed up against Cal with his mile-long legs and slender frame. The full line of their bodies connected, aside from the underwear, but Cal imagined slowly smoothing his hands down Owen's taut stomach beneath the elastic, grinding forward, and palming him until the kid begged for more. He couldn't do that yet, though. He had to wait for Owen to *ask*, which made it all the more thrilling.

"What next, Owen?" he whispered.

"Nothing. Just this."

Cal blinked, certain he'd heard wrong. "Just this?"

"Mmhm."

"*This* is all you want?"

"Y-yes...."

"Okay," Cal said quickly when he sensed the tension returning to Owen's body and heard the worry in his voice, but he didn't understand.

This kid was beautiful and sweet, a good cook, a good conversationalist when not falling over himself with embarrassment. What could possibly be the reason he needed an escort to snuggle? It wasn't Cal's place to ask. Still, he was curious.

Holding Owen securely, Cal offered tender strokes down his arm but no farther. Pressed his cheek to the back of Owen's neck but didn't kiss him. Willed his body to come down from its excitement and held Owen like he'd been asked. He didn't know what to say, but he would never go against a client's wishes.

It wasn't long before Owen's shoulders started to shake, a sniffle and sharp intake of breath breaking the quiet. Cal told himself not to recoil; he didn't want

Owen to think this wasn't okay, but he didn't know how to handle someone breaking down in his arms who wasn't his sister.

"I'm s-s-sorry." Owen's voice shook with his body. "I don't know why I'm... crying...."

All Cal could do was shush him, nuzzle closer, and let his hand travel past Owen's elbow down his forearm—

A flinch pulled Owen's arm out of reach. "S-sorry. Old injury. It's fine. It doesn't hurt."

It was not fine. Cal knew what this was now, and it hardened like cement in his gut. Someone had hurt Owen. Deeply. Even physically, judging by that flinch. What monster had damaged him so much to cause this, Cal wondered?

He shouldn't be the person anyone relied on, especially not when they were dealing with true, visceral trauma. Owen needed something more than *him*, a friend, a therapist, not an escort in his bed. But who was Cal to tell someone what they needed when Owen had asked for him?

When Owen pulled Cal's hand back to reconnect on his forearm like an apology, like *he* needed to apologize, Cal couldn't keep quiet anymore.

"You don't have to answer, but... why? Why this?"

"Because I'm alone," Owen said, small but steady, like he wanted someone to hear this, though it was clearly still easier facing away from Cal. "Because my friends and family are hundreds of miles away, and I needed something tonight no one else can give me. I've always been terrible at dating.

"There was someone... a long-term someone, but he never gave me this. He never let anything be on my terms. I'm lonely without him, but I'm scared to go out. I don't want to fall into that same pattern and end up with someone else who only wants to use me for sex. Sorry!" He started as if he'd said something terrible. "I don't mean—"

"I'm not offended, Owen." Cal cut off his default reaction to assume blame. "No one uses me for sex. I give it freely. There's a difference. If this is all you want, then this is all we need to do. But next time, you don't have to pay extra."

"I don't?"

"This isn't exactly what is meant by 'anything goes.'" Cal smiled against Owen's skin, and his tension eased away.

"Oh," he said through a chuckle. "Alyssa says it's Ugly Duckling Syndrome. I met *him* after I… blossomed, I guess? I was so used to being a gangly dork in high school that no one wanted, I didn't know how to have confidence with people once I was—and this is her talking not me—hot."

"You are hot. You're stunning."

"You're paid to say that," Owen murmured. Normally, when someone shot that phrase at Cal, he got angry, but Owen hadn't said it with any derision toward *him*.

"I'm paid to be here," Cal said, "but I say what I feel. Your terms. Your wishes. And I am happy to oblige. But when it comes to my opinion, I will always be honest with you."

After a moment, he didn't think Owen was going to respond, but then his voice filtered up with a softly whispered, "Thank you."

Owen's sniffles faded as Cal cuddled him close. Anything amorous between them tapered off, leaving only the quiet and two connected bodies lying in tandem.

Eventually Cal felt Owen's breathing steady and knew the kid had fallen asleep. He never slept with a client unless he was staying the night, and that hadn't been part of Owen's request. Cal figured he'd give him a few hours, but only twenty minutes passed before Owen stirred.

"Sorry!" he yelped as soon as he roused and shifted in Cal's arms to face him. He'd never taken his glasses off, so they sat askew now, and one side of his hair was flattened. "I didn't mean to fall asleep."

"You must have needed it," Cal said, cupping Owen's face to caress a thumb down his cheek, which brought out a fresh blush.

"You don't have to stay the night or anything." Owen leaned into his hand even as he averted his gaze. Then his eyes went wide. "Is that extra? If I ever wanted you to?"

"It is. Still less than 'anything goes.'"

"Right." Owen laughed, extracting himself from Cal's hold so he could sit up. He appeared refreshed and less shaky when he reached to fix his glasses. "Thank you. I feel a lot better now. I needed this. I know we've been dancing around the subject, but… could this be a regular thing? Do you do that?"

"I do that." Cal sat up next to him, unused to sharing a bed with a client when both of them still had an article of clothing on. "I'm very picky about who I take on as a regular, and I only have one available slot at the moment."

"Oh…." Owen looked dejectedly down at his lap.

"So absolutely, Owen." Cal stressed that he meant that as a yes. "We can do this again. Since you were accepted onto the roster, you have the direct line to my handler. Call her to set up the sort of schedule you'd prefer, and we can go from there. As long as I'm free, I can see you as many nights a week as you want—and can afford." He kept his tone light to put Owen at ease.

"Okay." Owen smiled so delightful and boyish. "I'll do that. I should let myself settle in more this weekend anyway."

They fell into simpler conversation after that as they got up and began to get dressed. Soon, Owen was walking Cal to the door, but he paused at the computer desk to write a note for him.

"For your wardrobe. Ask for Dennis. He has a good eye. Don't let the smugness deter you. Once he knows who you are and that you're willing to spend, he'll treat you well."

"Thanks. I'll... see you soon?" Owen asked, hovering after Cal on his way out, still unsure of himself and blushing scarlet.

*Scarlet*—Cal's newest name for the books.

"Looking forward to it."

He meant it. He meant everything he'd said to Owen during their evening together, but he had no idea what had possessed him to allow such a change to his routine. Cal never took on clients like Owen— he didn't think there *were* clients like Owen—but especially when this case meant that Cal might not be the healthiest outlet for him, yet he couldn't bring himself to disappoint Owen and turn him away.

Cal *had* said he needed a change. Maybe helping Owen was exactly what both of them needed.


**FALLING** against his door after Cal left, Owen couldn't stop grinning. He'd fallen asleep with a stranger who'd obviously been thrown by his requests, but he hadn't made a complete fool of himself. And it had been so long since Owen felt that content in someone's arms.

When he scheduled Cal for the night, he hadn't intended to make this ongoing. Money wasn't a problem, especially if Owen's needs fell under the normal fee for Cal's services, but he couldn't let this go on forever, just… a few more nights to help him with the transition, so he didn't freak out and call Harrison in a fit of desperation. Cal's company was preferable, and Owen could use him for a few events coming up, not always just to… snuggle.

He was a good snuggler, though, strong and warm and understanding. Owen wished he hadn't broken down like that, wished he hadn't flinched when Cal's touch moved to the arm Harrison had hurt, but with this first night out of the way, he already felt more comfortable in his own skin than he had in a very long time.

Owen might be out of his mind for hiring an escort on the regular for snuggle sessions and dinner dates, but Cal was like a dream, and Owen was not ready to wake up yet.

## Chapter Four

**THE** mayor was taking all of Owen's suggestions, even when his "people" insisted that some of the recommendations were "cost prohibitive."

"Is it going to bankrupt the city or this project in any way?"

"Well, no, but—"

"Then we do things Owen's way. He has the data, and we want this program to work. Will it cost us more or less money if we have to scrap the whole thing in three months because we cut corners and failed?"

"But Mr. Mayor—"

"Unless we absolutely can't make things work the way he's suggesting and you have the numbers to back that up, we do things his way."

It meant that all the training and equipment Owen recommended for the officers was being implemented before the program went live. It wouldn't be perfect—nothing could ever be perfect—but they'd have the highest chance for success to prove the system worked. That meant more funding when crime started to decline, more opportunities, and overall safer neighborhoods all over Atlas City.

It also meant that Owen didn't feel glued to the mayor's office, worried that something would go off the rails when he spent time at Nye Industries. He could relax. As much as he ever relaxed anyway.

Working with Frank and his team made Owen feel more like he belonged than overseeing the mayor's group. The mayor's people were more public relations officers. Frank was a fellow scientist. Right now, Owen was a contractor for the company, an outsider looking in, but Keri had promised him a full-time position if he wanted it. Still, Owen didn't want to decide anything long-term too quickly. For once, he was taking his time.

He'd been so focused at the start of the week, refreshed from his idyllic Friday night and a low-key weekend of organizing his schedule—and a little shopping, thanks to Cal—that he hadn't gotten too many new outfits. The man Cal recommended, Dennis, was a little smugger than Owen could handle in large doses. Plus, he wanted to fill out the rest of his wardrobe in Cal's company if he could.

It was Wednesday now, and Owen was seeing Cal tonight. He hadn't been able to concentrate all morning. His tension and loneliness had started to increase again, a little more each evening he came home to an empty apartment. Alyssa, Casey, and Mario helped a little, like they were tag-teaming to call him once a day to make sure he didn't break down and phone Harrison. Owen had no intention of doing that, but it seemed more manageable when he knew that tonight he had something to look forward to.

Cal was so handsome, so attentive and engaging, his touch sure and strong wrapped around Owen's body….

"You all there, Owen?"

"Huh?"

Owen looked up from the workstation they'd given him, where he was basically auditing all of the company's current and future projects for ways his models could benefit the research, or to see if he had any other epiphanies they might be interested in. A few times, he had assisted Frank's R&D team where they were stumped, already proving his worth, not that he'd been put on the spot. He just felt so at home in this type of environment. Right now, however, he was a little too lost in his daydreams.

"Sorry, Frank. Must need another dose of coffee." Owen smiled.

"I can get a fresh one for you, Mr. Quinn." An intern jumped up excitedly.

"That's okay, Rory. I need to stretch my legs anyway."

Excusing himself from the large laboratory, Owen slipped into the hallway to head to the nearest break room. He hadn't gotten around to buying an extra pair of glasses yet, but he wore one of his new blazers—charcoal this time instead of blue—over a darker charcoal sweater and slim black slacks. A little monochrome for Owen's tastes normally but much sharper than his usual looks.

He was so up in his head wondering if Cal would like the new outfit when they saw each other tonight, that he didn't realize he hadn't taken his used coffee cup with him to refill until he was about halfway to the break room, down a deserted hallway about to pass an opening down another hall—when a large hand gripped his left forearm and yanked.

Alarm bells went off in Owen's mind like a bullhorn, panic gripping his chest and phantom pain shooting up his arm as his breath caught and he told himself to *fight*. Don't let this happen again. *Fight back.* But he couldn't. He was too afraid, too immediately brought back to feeling small and trapped, that all he could do was gasp when his assailant pulled him into the corner and pushed him against the wall.

"M-Mr. Walker?" Owen stuttered.

As the owner behind that strong grip materialized, Owen realized the hold hadn't been rough and he hadn't been pushed back with any force, of course he hadn't. This was Adam Walker, CEO of Walker Tech, who'd been trying to schedule time to see Owen since last week.

The man would have been intimidating for his impressive height, also his powerful build and classic good looks, if not for his humbling nature.

"Please, call me Adam," he said brightly, as if he hadn't just seized Owen and brought him into a dark hallway. "Glad to finally meet you, Owen."

"Uhh… shouldn't that be happening at *your* building or over lunch somewhere?"

"Which you keep rescheduling on me."

"I-I haven't had time to—wait." Owen steadied himself and his breathing. He was *fine*. Adam hadn't intended to scare him, but this was also highly suspicious behavior. "Is this corporate espionage?" he hissed.

"Nonsense." Adam chuckled. "Think of it more like a game of tag. Or keep-away, seeing as how Keri has been keeping you away from me all week."

"I don't think she's purposely—"

"All in good fun, Owen." Adam patted his shoulder, sort of like the friendlier version of a high school quarterback who, in this case, would also have been captain of the chess team. "She wants first crack at you, I get it, but I have a proposal to make, and if I wait for your calendar to clear, you'll be knee-deep in projects here before we can get anything off the ground."

"O-okay." Owen might have been quick when it came to deciphering data, but he tended to be slow in social situations, especially when taken by surprise like this.

"What's she have you working on?" Adam asked.

"Oh, I can't—"

"It's the next generation of those chips of hers, right? I'm not asking you to give up any secrets. All I'm asking is for you to listen to my proposal for doing a joint venture with my nanotechnology and help me present it to Ms. Nye." He smiled with that wide, beaming expression again. Much like the mayor, he certainly seemed genuine for someone Owen probably shouldn't trust too easily. "Only if you like what I have to say, of course."

"Well… I guess I could *listen*," Owen said, trying to analyze the situation for any ways he might be in over his head or could get in serious trouble. "You've done joint projects before. But then… why can't you propose this to Keri yourself?"

"I've tried." Adam leaned back a step, finally giving Owen room to breathe. "I haven't been able to prove the data in a way her investors see as viable. But with your guidance, your models, I think we can make it work. Hear me out…."

Owen wasn't usually up for adventure like this, being secretive and squirreled away. His heart was beating rapid-fire the entire time, as he hid at the end of a hallway no one went down, listening to a multimillion-dollar CEO in the building of another multimillion-dollar CEO tell him how together they could change the world.

He was pretty sure this *was* corporate espionage, in a way, but as long as the end goal was for the benefit of both parties, it didn't seem like he was doing anything bad simply by listening, especially when it meant furthering medical technologies that could save lives on a whole other spectrum from what he was doing with the mayor's office.

Thinking of everything he could accomplish, he sort of felt like a superhero.

The proposal was fascinating, but Owen could see where the holes came in and why Adam and his scientists were stumped. It wasn't ready to be brought to Keri yet. Owen would need to think about this, see some of Adam's data first, and work on the models himself.

"I won't share anything with you about Keri's side, and I won't share anything with her about your side, but I need to use research from both to make this work."

"I'm putting a lot of faith in you, Owen." Adam nodded. "But the end results will be worth it if we can move forward on this together."

Owen hadn't signed anything with either company yet that prohibited him from doing something like this, but he *was* technically going behind Keri's back. He was terrified and excited at the same time. If this worked out, it was exactly the sort of thing he'd come to Atlas City to achieve.

He wanted to tell Alyssa, Casey, and Mario to get their opinions, but he couldn't risk leaving a phone trail.

Then he thought of *Cal.* He could gush to someone in person in only a few hours. Once he'd parted ways with Adam and continued to get his coffee, he couldn't wait for the day to be over.

The catch in his throat from how he'd been ambushed lingered, but only enough to leave Owen slightly shaken. He didn't blame Adam. He just needed to do something to help him overcome his instant panic reaction whenever someone touched his left arm. He certainly hadn't meant to flinch when Cal did it the other night.

Alyssa had suggested self-defense classes to build up his confidence, which he'd tried to start attending back in Middleton, but he hadn't really had time to keep it up. Along with all the other info Alyssa had gathered to help him settle into his new city, she'd included a gym that came highly recommended for that sort of thing, where Owen could get a personal trainer instead of having to do classes, which weren't really his scene.

Maybe he'd set something up before heading home today and give Knockback Gym a call.

*PRINCE* was an ideal client. Gorgeous. Wealthy enough to request Cal's services often, but not too often since she was also a busy woman. She wasn't a princess, not really, but an ambassador working in the city. Cal forgot which tiny country she was from, but she might as well have been royalty for how she carried herself.

She didn't have the time or patience for romance, but she had needs to fulfill, and Cal was the most efficient way to meet those needs without complication. She also liked to tie him up and play with all sorts of toys, but she was the type of dominating partner who knew how to treat her companion with respect and care. Cal wouldn't have put up with anything less.

Normally he saw Prince in the evenings, but she'd agreed to a schedule shift to accommodate his other evening plans—Owen Quinn.

"I appreciate you squeezing me in early."

"My pleasure, Calvin." The tall, Amazonian woman laughed lightly as she freshened up at the vanity mirror in her bedroom. "Or both of ours, I should say. A break in the afternoon is a nice treat on occasion. Busy man today, are you?"

Cal had nearly finished dressing, moving a little slower with the strain in his arms from being tied to the bedposts a few minutes ago. "Can I help it if I'm in demand?"

"Even the wicked need to rest, don't they?" She finished the application of bright red with a smack of perfect, bowed lips.

"It's not that kind of evening. Next week?"

"Certainly. I'll let Miss Tyler know what works best with my schedule." Standing to stop him in the doorway before he could leave, she mimed kissing both cheeks to spare him the stain of her fresh lipstick. "*Ta leme.*"

"Soon." Cal nodded.

He needed to shower and change before seeing Owen. Cal enjoyed his work, wouldn't do it if he didn't, so it surprised him how excited he was for the evening ahead, without the usual endgame.

Owen was in the system now, meaning his requests came to Cal's inbox like a normal email. *Remember how I can't cook anything besides that goulash? Maybe we should order in.*

Cal had messaged back a grocery list. *I'll teach you how to make something new tonight. Unless you had other ideas?*

*No! That sounds perfect.*

Cal arrived to find Owen looking even more delectable than he had the first evening, and far better dressed.

"Dennis holds up, I see," he said as Owen invited him in.

Owen's cheeks filled with color to solidify his codename when he glanced at his sweater. "Kind of a jerk, like you warned me, but I really like the things I got. This is good?"

"Very good." Cal had toned down his own wardrobe tonight, a white button-down with a cream sweatshirt and tan slacks, painting him more pastel than Owen's ensemble in gray.

"I need an extra pair of glasses next," Owen said, leading Cal to the kitchen, where he already had the groceries set on the counter. "I was thinking of something more delicate than my black ones for contrast. Maybe gold? Thinner frames?"

"I can picture that. Would you like company for another shopping trip?"

"Can we?" Owen filled with light when he got excited like it might burst from his pores.

"Absolutely. Perhaps this Saturday afternoon? I believe my schedule is free."

"*Great.* I'll send a request tomorrow. We can get lunch. But dinner first, right?" Owen glanced skeptically at the collection of ingredients waiting for them. "I'm a fast learner but a bit of a klutz. You may regret wearing light colors when we're working with pasta sauce, and it's probably best if I do minimal chopping. Though I guess we don't need to chop anything...."

"Not for this recipe," Cal said. "Ever learned how to make a good lasagna?"

Those large hazel eyes kept catching Cal off guard. "I figured that's what we were making from the noodles, but this seems different."

Cal's list had told Owen to get ground turkey instead of hamburger and spinach and sundried tomatoes to go with the ricotta filling. "My own recipe. The real secret is in the right cheese." He patted the bag of shredded whole-milk mozzarella, that he then realized was open with a few shreds spilled onto the counter.

"It's *really* good cheese," Owen said, scratching the back of his head to betray his embarrassment. "I may have stolen a few handfuls already."

He had no idea how charming he was without trying. "Well then, you've mastered step one of this meal." Grabbing his own handful, Cal devoured mozzarella from his fingers with unabashed enthusiasm.

Owen laughed. That scarlet blush was going to be their constant companion.

"I wrote down the recipe for you," Cal said. "All you have to do now is watch me, follow my instructions, and tell me about your day. Still settling in well?"

As Cal rolled up his sleeves to work, Owen mirrored him and eagerly fell into a fast-paced retelling of his week's highlights so far. Cal understood now what Owen needed from him—basic companionship. A warm body in his home. A friendly face around to listen and exist in his presence without obligations between them, besides Cal's fee. A *friend*, but more intimate than that when Cal was expected to undress and hold Owen close again at some point. Even the most open-minded of friends might not be up for that caveat to a new relationship.

There were times when Cal played the role of date with his clients. He'd cooked with them before too, but conversation rarely strayed to anything deep, and a "happy ending" was always expected, often the main attraction more than a meal. Owen flipped that on its head.

If this was one of Cal's other clients, he would have stepped up behind him while cooking and guided his hands until their pulses ratcheted and Owen's hips ground back against his own. But Owen didn't want to be seduced, so Cal remained at his side.

"You don't think I'm being taken advantage of, do you?" Owen asked once they had the lasagna in the oven and were slicing bread. They'd already opened a bottle of wine. Owen said he was a beer man too, so Cal decided that the next meal they shared would be paired with something lighter.

"You're the one in a position to take advantage," he said. "You could come to a conclusion with your models, take the research for your own, and screw over both companies."

"I'd never do that!"

Cal snickered at his scandalized expression. "I know. Just saying, you're not under any legal obligations, only moral ones. Nye and Walker are lucky they're dealing with you and not someone less scrupulous."

That seemed to be what Owen wanted to hear. He must have been used to being taken advantage of. "It's kind of fun," he said, walking the plate of bread to the table while Cal followed with their half-drunk glasses of wine. "Sneaking around, working on a side project like a spy or something."

"I'm glad you're enjoying yourself. Who knew data science could be so exhilarating?"

"It's not usually so clandestine." Owen chuckled. "But thanks for your input on the whole thing. I feel better after a second opinion. Adam seems so nice."

Adam Walker, possibly the richest man in the city, was *nice*. "You do realize how impressive it is that you're on a first-name basis with three of the most powerful people in Atlas City?"

Even when Owen's face scrunched, he looked endearing. "I don't think of it like that. They're all pretty down to earth."

Cal and Owen sat to enjoy more of the wine and a slice of bread, taking up the same seats as their first evening. "Don't get too comfortable with that being the case. They're rare breeds. A lot more people in their positions would be ruthless."

"I know." Owen nodded. "That's why I came here instead of staying in Middleton."

"Your past company had some villainous characters in it?"

There came that shadow over Owen's features again. "My ex. He took a lot of my ideas for his own, said they'd have more luck being accepted if they came from him since he was CTO. Which isn't entirely a lie," he added in a rush, maybe used to defending the man. "That did give the ideas more clout, but it took me a long time to recognize how much he was using me."

Cal burned with curiosity to press for more—a CTO in Middleton, a clear asshole, a man closer in age to Cal most likely—but the way Owen's shoulders drew up said he didn't want to be reminded of the past.

"You know what they say?" Cal raised his glass for a toast, and Owen brought his forward to clink. "The best revenge is living well."

Owen glowed as if he still didn't believe how well he was living.

The oven timer dinged, and Owen took in a deep breath. "That smells so *good*. I'm starved."

"Ah, ah, ah." Cal rose to follow him from the table. "It needs to rest before we dish up."

"For real?" Owen looked so crestfallen. He lived his life at breakneck pace, while Cal preferred to slow things down. "I was that kid who ruined pans of brownies because I couldn't wait for anything to 'rest.'"

"I never would have guessed," Cal teased. "Patience, Owen. All things in due time."

They settled in the kitchen after removing the pan from the oven, facing each other.

"Speaking of time," Owen said, "I knew it was only a matter of time before I started getting invites to bigger events. When Adam and I were talking, he invited me to this fundraiser in a couple weeks, a chance to hobnob with the right people and bring the different sides of my work together. I really should have a date." Bashful in the span of seconds, he glanced down at his twiddling thumbs. "I'm terrible in situations like that, so someone who can help me navigate being, you know… *normal* would be really appreciated. Would you come with me? Is that okay, or do we need to keep things more private—"

"I'd be delighted to accompany you, Owen," Cal said, having expected this eventually and unable to deny how eager he'd been. "Well timed for our shopping trip. How many suits do you own?"

"Like *full* suits? Coz it's more like blazers, and I don't really like ties…."

This young man was in desperate need of spit and polish. "You've been invited by Adam Walker to a fundraiser. You're going to need to wear a tie. Maybe even black tie?"

"Not black tie," Owen assured him. "I figured I could get away with—"

"You still need a tie," Cal scolded. "We'll find something comfortable for you. I bet you've never had

a suit tailored to your measurements before. You want
to impress these people, don't you?"

"Yes."

"Then I'll help you do just that in something you'll
love, I promise. But I should warn you." Cal hated to
bring this up, but he owed Owen the truth.

"Warn me?"

"I tend to avoid these types of events because
there is the chance some of my other clients might be
in attendance. Now," he continued when he saw the
concern enter Owen's face, "you signed the same forms
they did, they know not to call attention to me or what I
do, and I wouldn't expect any of them to, but if they see
us together, they will make assumptions."

"Oh." Owen relaxed. "I don't care about that.
Unless you do?" And he went right back to worried.

"I'm quite comfortable with who I am," Cal said.

"I never would have guessed," Owen mocked
back, then chuckled to himself before looking at Cal
sheepishly. "I know you can't answer this, but... you
don't have Adam or Wesley as clients, do you?"

"No. I can tell you plainly, that to my knowledge,
no one you're working with is a client of mine. But that
doesn't mean a fundraiser for Walker Tech won't come
with familiar faces."

"I get it. Not that I'm worried, but how do you
keep your clients anonymous anyway? You know my
real name. I assume you know everyone's real names."

"I don't refer to them as that in mixed company.
We use codenames for clients."

"You do?" Owen perked up. "Like what?"

Clearly, he had playing spy on the brain, but Cal didn't
want to embarrass him by admitting he'd dubbed him
"Scarlet" because of his blush. "I have one I call Narcissus."

*"Narcissus?"* Owen fell into giddy laughter. "That full of himself?"

Usually Cal didn't discuss clients with anyone outside of Rhys, but Owen's curiosity was harmless by comparison. "He has a mirror on the bedroom ceiling."

*"He does?"* Owen flushed with color, though the way his eyes darted down Cal's body proved he wasn't completely without interest.

"Then there's The Godfather," Cal said.

"Like… he's with the mob?"

*"She* is the daughter of a very cutthroat businessman, but I don't believe he has actual mafia ties. I certainly hope he doesn't." If Asher Morris was a mob boss in disguise and ever found out Cal was hired by his daughter for biweekly romps in the bedroom, he'd have his head on a chopping block in hours.

"She?" Owen asked, kicking at the kitchen floor with one of his sock-clad feet.

This always came up when Cal had a new client; they wondered if he had a "type" since he populated both sides of the Nick of Time website, but the things most people had a preference for didn't mean as much to him. As long as he felt drawn in, anyone could catch his interest.

"I tend to see more men than women, but I equally enjoy anyone's company. Does that bother you?"

"No." Owen was quick to answer. "Sorry, I shouldn't ask about other clients."

*Jealous.* Mildly maybe, but it was there. Many clients got jealous, but it stirred something different in Cal seeing it in Owen.

Daring to take a risk, he pushed forward and slid his hands overtop Owen's on the island counter, eliciting a gasp from the timid young man.

"When I'm with you, you are all I think about. I promise," Cal said and gently lifted Owen's hands to tug him toward the stovetop. "Now come on. Get the plates. I wouldn't want to torture you any further waiting for your hard-earned meal."

A giggle passed Owen's lips, his blush still on his cheeks as Cal's gamble paid off. Not that he wanted to push Owen for anything physical, but he hoped to get him more comfortable accepting what he offered even if that never went further than a cuddle.

What Cal couldn't admit yet was that when he'd been with other clients the past few days, often his thoughts had strayed to *Owen*.


**THE** lasagna tasted amazing, and it was a meal Owen could replicate, though there was something far more enjoyable about having made it with Cal. He wasn't filled with the same anxieties he'd experienced the first night they saw each other. If Cal was going to be put off by first impressions, he would have run for the hills and never returned.

Still, Owen wasn't sure how to segue from finishing another meal together to cuddling without sounding like a complete *dork*.

*Um, can we undress now?*

Urg.

A crack of thunder, almost loud enough to rattle the walls, made Owen jump and drew his attention to the windows and just how dark the clouds had become. He'd caught flickers of lightning a few times during dinner, but now he could see the storm in full swing, one of those impressive displays of sparring lightning shooting from one cloud to another in an endless dance.

"Afraid of storms?" Cal asked.

"I *love* storms," Owen said. Then with a surge of adrenaline, he leaped from his chair to pull Cal from the table and hurried them toward the balcony door. Cal had such an amazing, *deep* laugh. "Quick, before it starts to rain! I have a great view from here. Look." He pointed to the gap in the cityscape between the lights of Nye Industries and Walker Tech, where there was nothing but *sky* and flash after flash of lightning sparkling in the dark. "These are my favorite kinds of storms. Isn't it beautiful?"

Owen was so transfixed watching the skyline, he didn't feel Cal's gaze on him until he heard "Breathtaking" and realized Cal wasn't looking at the storm.

The heat filling Owen's face made it impossible to acknowledge the comment. When he dared sneak a peek, Cal had turned forward again, his face lit intermittently by bursts of light.

They stood on the balcony awhile, taking in the storm, the natural lightshow in the middle of a glowing city, quiet but content in each other's company—until another rumble of thunder heralded the start of the rain showers and they ducked back inside.

It made Owen giggle when Cal reached to take his glasses from him since they were speckled with raindrops. He took them back and set them on the end table rather than wipe them clean.

"Can we… umm…."

"Owen," Cal said, low and quiet, "you don't have to be nervous to ask for anything you want."

That just made Owen shiver harder. He focused on Cal's features, softened without his prescription. "Can we undress like last time but stay out here and lay on the sofa to watch the storm?"

The way Cal looked at Owen made him certain the other man wanted to undress him himself, but even if Cal was merely talented at playing a role and making Owen feel wanted, he knew he'd lose his nerve if he allowed that. So, he smiled when Cal nodded and backed toward the sofa to undress on his own. Cal didn't do as much of a striptease this time, but when he was down to his underwear, he lay back and beckoned for Owen to join him.

Pleasantly crushed between Cal and the inside of the sofa as he lay half on top of him, Owen settled into the snug contact to watch the lightning dance between the clouds.

"Thank you for this," he said.

"You don't need to thank me. This is what I'm here for."

"This isn't what you normally do though, right?"

"True. I don't have other clients like you." Cal hugged Owen closer, fingers trailing up his arm in soothing motions.

"So... *thank you*," Owen said again.

"You're welcome."

It was only later, when they'd dressed and Cal was leaving, that Owen realized he'd never asked what codename Cal had given him.

CAL'S schedule remained tight the next two weeks, but he always made time for Owen. When he took on a regular, he was only obligated to see them once a week. Some he saw closer to once a month per their own requests, but Owen asked for him frequently, and even when Cal had something else going on, he tried to accommodate Owen first.

It wasn't charity or pity. Seeing Owen more often was smart business and relaxing for Cal in ways no other client could provide. It was self-care as much as for Owen's benefit. Cal also enjoyed a challenge, and Owen's wardrobe was certainly that. He'd done well with Dennis, but he needed several more staples to round out his closet, including something stylish for the fundraiser and other upcoming events.

Cal picked out a burgundy three-piece suit for him that would make heads turn for sure, which Owen had protested until he saw himself in it with the first few pins in place to help it hug his frame.

"Are you sure? This isn't too… *flashy*? What will you wear?"

"Something more muted. You're the belle of the ball, Owen. The point is to make you stand out, and I'm merely an accessory."

"That's not very nice."

"It's not about nice. It's about playing the crowd. Trust me. A little drama will make a more lasting impression."

Owen would be wearing his new glasses as well: a gold pair like he'd wanted that was more fitting for fancy nights out.

Most evenings Cal spent in Owen's company they stayed in and made dinner. A few times Cal took Owen out—though Owen always paid. Occasionally they looked through Owen's furniture magazine or new ones Cal brought over so he could finish decking out his apartment with artwork and accents.

There was one larger piece Cal had pointed out that Owen immediately purchased, an impressive print with bold swaths of color, mostly blue and silver in the center with purple and red along the edges. "Like a snowstorm in a forest fire," Owen had said.

He had a good eye when he trusted himself to use it, but it warmed Cal how easily Owen took to his suggestions without shying from letting him know when he didn't like something.

The print was the centerpiece of Owen's living room wall now.

Whenever they were together, every meeting always ended with clothes shed and close contact snuggled on the bed or sofa. Never more than that, but there was never an encounter without it. Owen hadn't cried since the first night, but he clung to Cal sometimes like he couldn't anchor himself without him. Cal had to be careful not to become a crutch Owen wouldn't be able to move on from.

The fundraiser was swiftly approaching, which would help get Owen's feet wet to better ease into his new life, but it also put them in the public eye together. Assuming Owen would be nervous over this, Cal prepared the perfect cover if he didn't want to pass him off as his boyfriend.

"My publicist?"

"I'll be playing that role to some extent anyway, and no one will bat an eye."

"What if people think I'm *dating* my publicist?"

"No one will bat an eye at that either," Cal said. "They'll think you audacious. Then they'll meet you and fall for your charms. Your good work will only bolster their impressions after that."

Given how in demand Owen was and how much he was worth, he needed a publicist anyway. Who better than Cal, who knew exactly how to handle these sorts of people? He even took it upon himself to help Owen schedule interviews, answer emails, scan local media for press mentions they weren't expecting, and craft a social media presence, since Owen had only ever used Facebook and only for personal matters.

Cal had blocked off his schedule for the fundraiser the moment Owen invited him, but he'd been considering clearing the day after as well in case the evening ran long. Lara had called him into the office to rearrange his scheduling anyway, so he planned to see if *Narcissus* would be willing to push things back a day this week.

Before he could make the request, however, Lara handed him dismissal papers.

"Narcissus is removing *himself* from the roster? What for?"

She shrugged from where she sat behind her desk. "He and his ex are giving it another go. He sends his best. Left you a hefty bonus for the short notice. Shall I get you back in the catalog to fill the slot?"

"No," Cal said before he realized how quickly the response left him. Giving himself a moment to consider *what* he was thinking, he distracted himself by signing the forms.

"No?" Lara pressed.

"I've been extra spent lately. Scarlet is a demanding client." Cal hadn't told Lara or anyone outside of Rhys what he and Owen got up to when they met, but she couldn't deny his full schedule lately.

"Demanding, huh?" She eyed him when he handed the forms back to her like she could read between every line he ever used. "And he looks so unassuming in that selfie."

"I never kiss and tell," Cal said, considering he and Owen had never kissed. "Send him a note so he knows I'm free the day after the fundraiser."

"In case he wants you to spend the night?"

Cal hadn't considered that, but now that Lara had mentioned it, he wondered. "Make the offer, but don't push if he doesn't bite. I'm sure Dick won't mind me reducing my client load given the number of days Scarlet's been booking me."

"Your call, Calvin."

Technically Cal had the space to add another client, but the idea of adding anyone new didn't sit well with him, and he always went with his gut.

If Owen took advantage of his more open schedule, Cal certainly wouldn't mind.

**OWEN** had been sleeping restlessly for days. He was so excited for the fundraiser, mostly to get the first of these events out of the way, though he was thankful Cal would be with him.

His work had been paying off with his side project for Adam, enough that they planned to bring the idea to Keri at the event, sort of like a friendly ambush, which seemed like a normal occurrence for the head of Walker Tech. From then on things were going to pick up as the police program went live soon too.

Grinning at his newest email, Owen wondered if he should agree to book Cal to stay the night after the fundraiser. He'd need decompression time, and Cal's arms were the ideal place to accomplish that. It wasn't that much extra to keep him until morning. Owen knew how to budget his time with Cal so it was hardly a detriment to his finances.

He worried about his self-control sometimes when Cal was wrapped around him. It was easy to forget that he wasn't allowed to *kiss*. Well, he *was*. He could have. He could change the nature of their time together with a single request. But that would ruin everything. The next time Owen kissed someone, he didn't want it to be business, even if Cal was a good friend and the most alluring man Owen had ever had in his bed.

Maybe their relationship wasn't only business to Cal, but Owen knew better than to get his hopes up. Cal was a *temporary* balm to ease the wounds he'd suffered, not a permanent solution to his loneliness.

He was midsentence typing a response to Cal's handler that yes, he *would* keep Cal through the night, when another email populated. Wondering if it might be an update from the agency, he clicked on the new message without finishing his draft.

It wasn't from Nick of Time Escort Service or Cal's direct account. It was from Harrison, with a blank subject line and the simple message:

*I miss you. Can we talk?*

Owen slammed his laptop closed.

## *Chapter Five*

**OWEN** didn't believe in violence unless there was no other option—partially because, up until a couple weeks ago, he didn't know how to throw a punch. His trainer from the Knockback Gym was teaching him more than basic self-defense, which Owen had been thriving off since his first lesson, even though the last thing he wanted was to punch someone's teeth in.

Especially when, today, he couldn't stop picturing Harrison's face.

"Watch your form, Owen," Lorelei said, holding the punching bag tightly as he pummeled it. "Good. Much better. I think this is the first day I haven't had to tell you to go harder."

Owen huffed, half out of breath and half in laughter. "Yeah, I… have a lot of pent-up energy today."

"Use it," she said, smiling supportively, her blonde hair pulled back into a ponytail, face sheened with sweat like his. She was the type of girl who cleaned up like a dream but had biceps bigger than Owen's. If he liked women, he would have had a serious crush on her. "Nice. Stop there. Let's do a few more defense moves before we call it a day."

Owen had been seeing Lorelei three to five times a week, usually in the mornings before work. His previous experience in Middleton meant he recalled the basics quickly enough, so she'd asked if he wanted to include additional training. Owen was glad he'd accepted. The workout cleared his mind before heading to the office, and successfully learning or completing a new move made him feel like he could take on anything.

Maybe even his ex, who'd risen like a zombie from the grave with his recent messages—*plural.*

The updates Owen had been making to his wardrobe meant he had been using old T-shirts for workout clothes, today being his favorite Spider-Man shirt and a pair of sweats. The gym itself wasn't anything too large, more for personal training like he was doing or sparring in various fighting styles. There was also a shooting range, something Owen planned to take advantage of once he felt comfortable enough with hand-to-hand, but he liked watching the kickboxing matches most.

He and Lorelei had a corner of the gym all to themselves. After moving to the center of their mat, he stood normally rather than in a fighting stance.

"Most attacks won't come when you expect them" had been Lorelei's first lesson.

She came at him from the front, and Owen deflected. Came from the side, and he twisted her to the floor. Came from behind, and he flipped her over his shoulder. All these moves were practiced now and simple enough to execute, because he knew what was coming.

"A couple more from each side," she said, but as Owen readied himself, trying to gauge which side she'd attack from next, she didn't make the move he anticipated but went straight for his *left arm*.

Owen seized up when her hands took hold of him, tensing all over, breath coming short, as he tried to remember how to counter being grabbed this way but he couldn't *think*—and then he was on his ass.

His bruises were minor compared to what his ego just suffered.

"What do I keep saying?" Lorelei said as she hefted him back to his feet.

"I know. I have to be able to counter even when you don't warn me."

The owner of the gym had encouraged Owen to be honest about his reasoning for training when he was assigned to Lorelei, and Owen had admitted much more than he expected to the kind woman who lent an ear as easily as she knocked him around the mats. Owen's main goal was to overcome the sensitivity associated with his left arm, not just to defend himself in a big city. When they'd first started sparring, she always warned him before attacking that part of him, but not anymore.

"You'll get there. Being vigilant for something that catches you off guard isn't easy."

Owen nodded, thinking of what his mother used to say. "Meet every surprise in life like you had a plan all along."

"Sound advice." Lorelei gently took his arm and squeezed reassuringly—part of the training, to always give positive attention after he'd been thrown into panic mode.

"Too bad I suck at following it," Owen said.

"You're one of my fastest improving students. Don't be so hard on yourself. I see a lot of abuse victims who want to push past their trauma. It can take months to be where you want to be. You've improved incredibly after only a couple weeks."

"I'm not really an abuse victim." Owen shifted his gaze to the floor. "It was only one time, one injury—"

"Owen, trauma isn't measured by *quantity*," Lorelei said firmly. "And abuse can be more than an injury. Your experience is no less valid than anyone else's. That's why you're here, right?"

"Right."

"Then let's go again." She squeezed his arm once more before releasing it.

The chime of Owen's cell phone drew his attention. He hated being *that guy*, but tonight was the fundraiser, and he kept waiting for something to go wrong. "One sec," he said in apology and dashed over to his gym bag to check his messages.

It was another email—from Harrison.

*Please, Owen. Just one phone call.*

Deleting the message like the others, Owen took Lorelei's advice and channeled his anxiety into something he could use. He ended up on his ass again after rejoining her on the mat, but he wasn't deterred.

"Again."


**CAL** didn't always have expensive taste, sometimes all he wanted was a burger and a chocolate shake, but today he was taking Rhys out for something lavish.

"Thought I owed *you* our next meal," Rhys said as they waited for their table. This place had the best steak in Atlas City, and since Cal didn't want to eat much before the fundraiser tonight, he needed a hearty lunch.

"You do, but today I feel like celebrating." Taking out his cell phone, he showed Rhys his most recent text thread from Claire.

Balloons and confetti emojis accompanied the message: *Dad didn't make parole.*

"I'll drink to that," Rhys said. "Screw your old man. What was he in for again?"

"Trying to fence stolen goods—to an undercover detective."

"Not even a good thief, huh?"

"Not a good anything."

Cal had left Middleton before his father went to jail, but he'd happily declined being a character witness when the request came through.

His father staying behind bars wasn't the only reason he had to celebrate, though. It had been a few days since he'd last seen Owen, and he hadn't shown off his suit for the event yet. Besides being muted to complement Owen's burgundy look, Cal was shooting for jaw-dropping again.

"What's that you said back to Claire?" Rhys asked before Cal could put his phone away.

"Just that if she grabs a drink tonight, she could try a place called Impulse."

"How do you know bars in Middleton anymore?"

"It's Scarlet's sister's," Cal said as if that should be of no consequence. "If she's as talented in her profession as he is in his, Claire will thank me for the recommendation."

Rhys eyed him as if there was something left unsaid— which there *wasn't*. Not that he'd admitted to himself anyway. "You still playin' vanilla with this kid?"

"I am a slave to my client's wishes." Cal gave a mocking bow.

"He not interested in that sorta thing?"

"He's interested, just... damaged." And far too good a man to be as damaged as he was. "Looking for something he can't get elsewhere, that's all."

"It's like you got yerself a housewife while you see yer mistresses on the side."

"Don't call him a *housewife*," Cal snapped. "And the difference is, he knows about my mistresses and doesn't care."

"Some married couples are like that."

"You got a client with that arrangement?" Cal recalled an earlier conversation the moment he said it. "Oh right, *Frost*, wasn't it?" Named for being an ice queen in conversation, not frigid between the sheets.

"Nah." Rhys glanced away. "I was wrong about her. Thought she was two-timin' her husband, but turns out he's not in the picture anymore."

"Divorcee?"

"Widow."

That gave Cal pause. Rhys's voice rarely dropped to such a gentle timber. "Sounds more personal than you like to get. Something I'm missing?"

"She's a good client," Rhys said with a sharp turn of his head. "Whadda ya pushin' for?"

He *liked* her. That was new. "Karma is a funny thing, my friend."

"The hell's *that* supposed to mean?"

Cal's name being called saved him from explaining. "Nothing. Come on, let me buy you a beer."


**OWEN** kept telling himself it would not be preferable to spontaneously combust, but between Harrison stalking him and the imminent fundraiser, he was certain something would implode.

He'd showered after his training that morning, but he'd still had the urge to be *cleaner* after work before he changed into his suit. Now he was running late.

His phone chimed, catching his attention from the bathroom. Hurrying out to check it still wearing only a towel, he wondered briefly if anyone could see him through his windows. There was an email from Cal sent a few minutes ago, saying he was on his way, but the newest message was Harry again.

*I'm so proud of you. I want to know how you're doing in Atlas City. Please answer me.*

Owen had been trying so hard to stay strong, but he could only take so much whittling at his resolve. Sinking down at the desk, he held his phone tightly in both hands while staring at his laptop. He'd barely opened it the past few days, as if it mattered whether he saw these messages there instead of his phone.

He had to get up and finish getting ready before Cal arrived, but for all his bolstering and forced bluster, he felt nailed to the spot.

Would it be so terrible if he answered, even if just to tell Harrison to leave him alone?

The phone ringing nearly toppled him out of the chair.

"Mario?" he answered.

"Hey, O, it's me."

"*Casey.*"

Alyssa had probably told him to call. She and Mario were more the psychic ones when it came to his well-being, not that Casey hadn't been there for Owen on numerous occasions. He'd just known him a shorter time, and Casey was far less invasive than the other two.

"I've been trying to stay calm, but I am *freaking out right now*," Owen said. "I don't know what to do. What should I do?"

"Calm down. What's going on?"

"You know what's going on. You can't tell me Alyssa hasn't filled you in."

There was a pause before Casey came back guiltily, "Okay, she has, but I thought maybe you'd want to start over like I didn't already know."

"Not really."

"Harry's being a dick."

"He's messaged me ten times in *two days*." Owen sagged into his chair. "How did he get my new email address? I changed everything. Got a new number. Even moved to a new city. Why does he have to do this now?"

"To get exactly this reaction," Casey said with endless patience, "because everyone knows how well you're doing without him. I just wish you had someone there with you."

A knock at the door startled Owen even more than his ringing phone, succeeding in upsetting him from the chair, though he managed to stumble to his feet. "Just a sec!" he called. It had to be Cal.

"Who's that?" Casey asked, as Owen stood frozen with indecision between hanging up, going to the door, and heading to his bedroom to put on clothes. "Wait, *do* you have someone? Alyssa didn't mention anything—"

"She doesn't know."

A pregnant pause replied before Casey said, "Oh, Owen, don't tell me that."

"It's nothing bad," Owen said, keeping his voice low. "It's... an escort I pay to spend time with me, which was sort of Alyssa's idea in the first place, but don't tell her I hired him and have been spending several nights a week with him."

This time the pause on the other end lasted a good ten seconds before Casey answered, "You remember I have no ability to lie to my wife, right? I crumble, O, humiliatingly. I'm almost as bad of a liar as *you*."

That would have been a jab if it wasn't true.

"You're sleeping with a prostitute?" he hissed.

"He's not a prostitute," Owen defended, then had to admit, "I mean, he is technically, but I'm not sleeping with him. We just have dinner and talk and cuddle on the sofa. It's… totally pathetic. Please don't tell Lyssa."

"Owen? Is everything okay?" Cal's voice called through the apartment door.

"Just one more second!" Owen called back before lowering his voice again. "Casey, I need him right now. He makes things easier, all this mess with Harry, I… I feel like I can handle it when he's around, but if Lyssa knows, she'll want to *talk* about it, and I can't do that right now."

"Mario doesn't know either?" Casey asked.

"Not yet. Just please? Tell her I have friends who are helping and I'm trying to stay calm. I won't let Harry get to me. I won't answer his emails. I'll be fine."

"Okay," Casey said with some reluctance, "but I'm calling again tomorrow after this fundraiser thing to make sure you're doing better. Got it?"

"Thank you." Owen sighed in relief, finally trudging toward the door. "I gotta go."

"Love you, pal. Never forget that."

"Love you too."

Owen hung up just as he yanked the door open, not really remembering he was practically naked and not wearing his glasses until he saw the way Cal's eyes raked down his body.

"Sorry!" he huffed in a fluster of shortened breath, taken just as off guard by Cal's appearance because his suit was simple and sharp but *all black*, and he was wearing black-framed *glasses* as if he'd stolen them right from Owen's bathroom.

**"YOU'RE** wearing glasses." Owen gaped at him.

Cal hardly thought *his* appearance was the focal point right now. "You're wearing a towel."

"Right!" Despite having seen each other in their underwear for weeks, Owen instantly became more self-conscious. "Sorry! I… uhh…." He started to back up, abandoning his doorway.

Taking the initiative to enter and close the door behind him, Cal took stock of Owen's appearance more carefully and noticed the phone in his hand. "What happened?"

"*Nothing*." Owen's eyes darted to the phone before he brought it to his chest like hiding a piece of evidence. "My brother-in-law. It's fine. I just—"

"Owen—"

"I'm sorry I'm not dressed yet—"

"We have plenty of time for you to get dressed. What's *wrong*?"

A deep breath left Owen, and he shook his head, not to deny Cal an answer but as if he needed to shrug off the automatic response to keep his troubles to himself. Bringing his phone up, he furiously swiped through screens, which confused Cal at first until Owen thrust the phone at him.

Gently accepting it, Cal looked down to discover Owen's deleted emails, which were currently dominated by message after message from the same man—Harrison Marsh. The nature of the emails made it obvious who he was.

"This is him?" Cal asked anyway.

Owen nodded, a tall, lanky bundle of tension with distress all over his face. "He got my new email somehow. He won't leave me alone. It's just so... I-I *c-can't*...."

Cal projected his movements as best he could so Owen had all the time in the world to slink away, but when he didn't so much as flinch, Cal hooked an arm around his shoulders to pull him close.

"What did he do to you?" Cal asked what he'd been holding back for weeks.

Owen choked on the tears he'd been trying to keep down and sank against him. "He's in my head, and I can't stand it. I keep having to tell myself not to respond, when I know even thinking about doing that is insane."

It took Cal years to get past the same thing with his father, past not being able to help loving someone but still knowing they're toxic. "Come here," he said, pulling Owen to the sofa to sit down. After placing the cell phone on the coffee table, he hugged Owen to his side, head tucked in the crook of his shoulder because he knew how much easier it was to talk without looking at someone. "You can tell me if you want. *Only* if you want."

Another breath shuddered out of Owen to stifle his tears as he sat at Cal's side with damp hair and a towel around his waist. "I feel so weak acting like this. I've been better. I've felt so much stronger. I hate that he can still do this to me."

"You are strong," Cal said. "He doesn't have power over you, other than what you give him."

"I know. But he did have power once. For a long time."

Slowly, as Owen eased into describing the relationship that led to the night he left his ex for good, Cal pictured it all unfolding like a vivid movie in his mind, with Harrison unfairly taking on the visage of Cal's father.

Cutting words to bring Owen down, but not blatant, more underhanded and passive, which made them dig so much deeper for their subtlety.

Kind words and touches only when it suited him.

An easily ignited temper, while being just as quick to apologize and make promises he never followed through on.

Making Owen feel worthless while he took his research for his own.

Knowing how and when to give Owen a night all about him so he felt wanted and stirred to passion.

Then night after night without tenderness, *taking* until he was satisfied.

It's no wonder Cal's mother left a similar man, but Cal pushed those thoughts aside, because this wasn't about him. He was here for Owen, and he wanted to be everything Owen needed in ways his father always told him he *failed* at.

*You're not good enough.*

*You'll never be good enough.*

Owen heard the same mantra, and it infuriated Cal to be on the outside looking in.

"He'd never been violent before," Owen said, softer now, but speaking freely, "just broke me down, little by little, years of being only good enough for him to keep me. Then after he'd get upset and lash out and needed to apologize, suddenly I was the best thing that ever happened to him.

"I'd been saving up the energy to give him an ultimatum for weeks. He'd gotten home late and was all over me. I said I wasn't interested, that I wanted to *talk*, but he kept pushing, kept trying to touch me and shut down the conversation, so I said if he wouldn't stop and listen then I was leaving.

"He... g-grabbed my arm to keep me against the wall, said I couldn't just *leave*. I told him I couldn't do this anymore, but the more I struggled, the more things escalated—him yelling and squeezing my arm, me begging him to listen and let go. He shook me and twisted my arm like he didn't care how much he was hurting me.

"I finally wrenched out of his grip, pulling so hard, I tripped and dislocated my elbow because he *wouldn't let go*. My forearm hurt worse, though. Stress fracture, I just didn't know it yet.

"He changed like a switch being flipped. All of a sudden, he was so sorry, swearing he'd make it up to me, like he always said, like he always *lied*. I don't remember grabbing anything or leaving the apartment. It was a haze until I got to my sister's.

"Harry tried for weeks after that to talk to me, but Alyssa is pretty protective, and every time I wanted to cave, she asked if I really wanted to go back to him. I didn't. I haven't seen him since. He wasn't my direct boss, so he couldn't fire me. I worked from home until I left Orion.

"It had finally *stopped*," Owen said with more force, for once betraying anger more than grief or fear. "Then I moved and thought I could put all this behind me. Now he's back, and I c-can't...." But even anger dissolved into tears sometimes, and Owen sniffled as he pressed his face to Cal's side. "I'm sorry. You smell so good, and I'm crying all over your suit."

Cal chuckled, forever caught off guard by how sweet this boy could be. "I'm fine. And you will be too. Do you want to skip tonight?"

"I *can't*."

"Then how about we take our time getting you relaxed and ready, and at worst, we'll be fashionably late?" Reaching with the hand not secured around Owen's waist, he tentatively slipped his fingers up Owen's forearm—the *left* arm he favored, which was obviously the one Harrison had hurt. It had to be a sign of Owen's trust in Cal that he snuggled closer rather than withdrawing. "Would you like me to help you relax?"

"I-I don't…." Owen went rigid.

"I mean a massage."

"Oh. That… that could be nice. Sorry."

"You don't need to apologize. Here. Face the window. It's a nice night."

Helping Owen sit up, Cal guided him to turn toward the cityscape, giving him the chance to rein in his tears before they faced each other again. The tension in Owen's shoulders was *criminal*. Harrison had done a number on him, in the past and in the past few days, using only a handful of emails to crumble the pieces of Owen's self-worth that he had fit back together while rebuilding his life. The least Cal could offer was the firm press of his fingers—since he couldn't drive to Middleton and punch Harrison Marsh in the jaw. Not tonight anyway.

The impromptu massage was made all the easier by Owen already being naked from the waist up. He was the one who smelled divine, like fresh mint from his shower.

"You are a remarkable man, Owen," Cal said, circling his thumbs deeply along Owen's shoulder blades and spider-walking up his neck. Every so often, the most delicious whimper would leave him. "Selfless, intelligent, *beautiful*. And so brave."

"Brave?" Owen repeated, then gasped when Cal found a stubborn knot.

"You came to a new city, dropped yourself in the middle of the unknown with a whole new career and strangers all around you. *That* is brave. You're also brave for leaving something that had gotten very good at drawing you back in."

Cal placed both hands on Owen's shoulders and firmly squeezed, then worked down his arms. He could see Owen in the reflection of the window in front of them, dim and indistinct, gaze unfocused even as he stared at the city, but as young and fragile as he looked, there was something powerful in the rawness of him laid bare without his glasses.

"Sometimes... I feel like I ran away," Owen said.

Cal ran once too, and he was happier for it. "Sometimes running is the brave thing."

There, at last, the stiffness in Owen's shoulders began to dissipate. They drooped, his neck lolling comfortably as he relished Cal's caresses. It was when he shifted how he was sitting to give Cal better access down his spine that the towel loosened at his hip, falling open to reveal a pale peek of naked thigh.

If this were any other client, Cal would have taken advantage of the opportune moment, but Owen wasn't *any other client*.

"Better get dressed now," he said, smoothing his hands up Owen's back and patting gently at his shoulders. "Your towel's come undone."

"Huh?" Owen glanced down, half dozing until he saw the exposed stretch of skin. "Sorry!" He twisted around to face Cal rather than grab the edges, which caused the towel to slip farther free, revealing the entirety of his thigh before he clambered to hold the cloth in place. As he looked at Cal with wide, clear eyes, regardless of the tears he'd shed, their faces were left dangerously close after all that scrambling.

Cal's hands had fallen from Owen's skin, but he reached now to hold the boy's cheek like he had their first night together. *Scarlet* colored Owen's skin.

"I sh-should… get ready."

"Mmm."

"Thank you," Owen said, placing his own hand over Cal's. "For listening. I won't let him ruin tonight. You worked so hard to make sure I'll look like a grown-up."

Laughter sputtered from Cal's lips before he could stop it, and Owen tumbled into laughter with him. Both their hands dropped, and after grabbing his towel to keep it closed, Owen stood.

"I'll be quick. *Fashionably* late."

"I'll be waiting," Cal said.

It *was* quick, considering the brief sound of a blow-dryer and the faint swearing at unruly hair, before Owen returned in his burgundy suit. Clean-shaven, stylish gold glasses in place, he was the picture of youthful decadence, while being entirely wholesome deep down—just what Cal had been going for to keep everyone at the fundraiser enamored.

"Are those real?" Owen asked, as if he'd forgotten he meant to inquire about Cal's glasses the moment he arrived.

"I normally wear contacts, but yes. Not a fan?"

"They're *wonderful*," Owen gushed, restored and alive with energy. "You look really good in them."

Jaw-drop accomplished yet again. "I thought I'd complement you better this way as part of your… payroll."

"As my *publicist*, you mean?"

"Exactly. Shall we?" Cal offered his arm, which Owen took with a playful giggle. "Let's knock 'em dead, Scarlet."

"Scarlet?"

*Shit.* Cal hadn't meant to say that. He'd never tripped up and called a client by their codename or vice versa, unless he was talking with Lara over private channels. "I... um...."

"I like it!" Owen said, after his expression went from inquisitive to understanding to lighting up with delight. "It's not *wrong*. Especially not right now." He nodded at his *scarlet* suit.

Cal never should have worried. Owen had started by surprising him and continued to again and again. "You'll feel on top of the world tonight. I promise."

**THE** fundraiser was at Atlas City Gardens, the type of venue people booked for weddings. Owen was in awe the moment they stepped inside, easily ushered in since he was a premiere guest.

The building was a several stories tall glass dome, like a greenhouse, filled with flowers and trees and currently lined with tables around an open space for mingling.

The event itself was to raise money for a charity close to Walker Tech's heart, the Society for Cancer Cell Gene Therapy. Adam raised money for all sorts of similar charities since that was his nanotechnology's focus. He'd steered his company in that direction after his wife survived breast cancer.

"Owen!" Adam pounced on them at the door. "Meet my wife, Teresa. And who's this?" He turned immediately to Cal, who didn't fumble for a moment.

"Cal White, Owen's publicist. Pleasure to meet you, Mr. Walker."

"Please, call me Adam."

Owen was too flabbergasted by Adam's whirlwind to shake Teresa's hand properly, though he offered a weak smile when he realized how flustered he was being. "S-sorry, I—"

"So nice to meet you, Owen." She saved him. "Don't mind Adam. He catches everyone off guard like that. Champagne?" She nodded at a passing waiter.

Owen was thankful for alcohol in that moment. For as beautiful and large as the gardens were, the place was packed with people in every direction, leaving barely any room to breathe. He wasn't used to being surrounded, no matter how fancy or vibrant the mob.

"I didn't realize you *had* a publicist," Adam said, not suspicious, just inquisitive.

"I'm not good at this sort of thing by myself," Owen said; Cal's lie was easy to maintain because most of what they told people would be the truth. "Everything will get so much more public and busy soon. I figured I needed the help."

"Smart thinking," Adam said. "Enjoy the party, Cal. And Owen, just mingle and relax for now. I'll find you when it's a good time to spirit away our friend Ms. Nye." He winked before disappearing into the crowd, pulling his wife along with him.

Owen took a healthy gulp from his champagne.

"Now let's see…." Cal scanned the room like an apex predator looking for a thrill. "There are at least five people in my sightline you'd benefit from meeting. Don't worry about a thing. I'll do all the introductions. You just have to smile and follow my lead. Ready?"

It was like the first day of school, the first day on a new job, a blind date, and being at the wrong end of a shooting gallery at the same time. But Cal's confidence and comforting grip on Owen's elbow pushed down some of the warring nerves in his stomach.

If he made a fool of himself, at least Cal was there to sweep up the carnage.

"Ready."

Cal didn't personally know any of the people they met, but he knew them by reputation, what circles they ran in, and where Owen's work might be of interest. He insinuated himself so smoothly, drawing Owen forward to introduce him and picking up on sentences Owen dropped as if their playing off each other had been planned, overall making Owen feel so at ease that he was soon holding his own.

Cal's hand was always there to support him, at his elbow or the small of his back, replacing his champagne with a fresh glass or snagging him an hors d'oeuvre. He was so charming; everyone took to him and gave Owen their attention that much more because of it. No real publicist could have done better.

Wesley was there with Keri, the type of event neither could afford to miss. By the time Owen and Cal circled the floor and happened upon the mayor and CEO, Owen was the one hurrying forward to make introductions.

"I thought Owen was settling in better," Wesley said as he patted Cal's shoulder. "Good to see he hired someone. Would I know any of your other clients?"

"More than likely," Cal said but didn't elaborate.

The evening was a resounding success, especially when Adam timed his ambush to right when Owen was in Keri's company and they stole her away, leaving Cal to chat with Wesley and Teresa. Cal hardly seemed put out in the company of the mayor and a woman who Owen had heard was on every nonprofit board in the city.

They pitched their idea to Keri, with Owen apologizing profusely for going around her. He held it together, though, since he could back the plan with workable models, enough that even though she gave Adam a look like they were high school glee club rivals and he'd just hit a high note she couldn't ignore, she agreed to a formal meeting the following week.

"You're more opportunistic than I expected, Owen. Nice job."

"Uh... thanks!"

Adam insisted on getting Keri a stronger drink to celebrate, but Owen excused himself to rescue Cal—or so he said, even if he actually just missed the man's company. It wasn't as daunting making his way through the throng as it might have been when they first arrived. A few people who Owen had already met smiled, and some new people stopped him to introduce themselves but were quick to let him move on.

Wesley and Teresa were being pulled in different directions when Owen spotted Cal, which spotlighted him in the aftermath of their departure, making it that much easier for Owen to take in how handsome he looked. The evening really was perfect.

Until Owen saw Harrison over Cal's shoulder, watching from afar.

Terror spiked through his veins like a shot of adrenaline, halting his breath and forward momentum. But it *wasn't* Harrison. It was just a man about his same age, height, and coloring, who happened to be looking in Owen's direction. So much for sloughing off the man's presence. He *could* be banished, though, and one day forgotten, Owen believed that, especially as his eyes met Cal's across the room.

"You okay?" he asked when Owen reached him.

"Fine. The pitch went *great*. I'm just losing my mind a little. I noticed someone watching me and thought it was Harrison."

Cal peered over his shoulder to see who Owen meant, but instead of coming back with a smirk and a tale about how the man was another competitor of Walker and Nye hoping to steal Owen away, his expression went cold. "He's not looking at you."

"A client?" Owen whispered.

"*Former*, or I'd have kept that information to myself, but this one I don't trust. I better head this off. Will you be all right?" He turned to Owen fully to cater to him first, even though he was clearly the troubled one this time.

A minute ago, Owen would have believed he *would* be fine, but after seeing a ghost from his past who turned out to be a ghost from Cal's, he wasn't sure anymore.

"Hey, Owen!" Frank's voice cut through the din.

Whirling around, Owen saw the tall, dark man approaching with a slighter, smiling man beside him.

"I can finally introduce you to Paul." He brought his husband forward. "See, not a figment of my imagination. He really is this handsome."

Owen had to laugh. "Hi! And here I was certain Frank was exaggerating. Nice to meet you, Paul." The tension eased with Frank and Paul's arrival, though the touch of Cal's hand at Owen's hip helped more.

"Sorry to slip away, gentlemen." He nodded to the pair. "Owen, I'll be right back. Then you can introduce me to your friends. Okay?"

"O-okay," Owen said, but even though he mourned the loss of Cal, he was more worried *for* him.

**MERLIN** stood beside an imported and impressive palm tree that had been cleverly hiding him from most people's view. He was a stock trader by day, nothing out of the ordinary, nothing shady, or at least not any shadier than the other businessmen here. He was attractive, all things considered—expensive suit, sly smirk—and waited for Cal with that smirk in place while sipping on champagne.

Of all the potential clients, past or present, who might have shown up tonight, Merlin was the only one Cal considered trouble.

"The new blood's cute, Calvin. A little young, though, don't you think?"

"Hardly the youngest on my calendar," Cal said. The Godfather was twenty-two, and Piper wasn't much older than Owen.

Insinuating himself beside Merlin to keep the conversation private, with a wall at their backs and the large palm beside them, Cal and his undesirable companion had one of the better views in the room.

"I hope your lawyer is in attendance," he added as he watched the crowd.

Merlin chuckled, hardly an easy man to intimidate. "Calm down. I'm not here to make a scene. I was invited."

"I'm sure you were."

"I'm hurt, of course, that you decided to end our time together. You were... exceptional." He cast a telling gaze down Cal's body. "But I understand. What I don't understand is why you thought it necessary to blacklist me from the entire agency."

Cal reveled in the bitterness of the man's tone. "I don't know what you mean."

"Everyone I attempt to book is 'unavailable,'" Merlin sneered. "I know when I'm being given the runaround. I've been flagged."

"There are plenty of other agencies in Atlas City. Pester one of them."

"I prefer yours."

"*Pity* then." Cal looked at him sharply. "We're rather full up these days."

The laughter from Merlin was menacing now, amazed at Cal's daring. "You think you're so untouchable because I signed a contract? Whispers are hard to prove but can be so damaging." He looked out at the crowd once more, focusing none too subtly on *Owen*. "Especially when someone is young and uninitiated in these shark-infested waters."

"You don't want to play that game, Sterling." Cal used his name with venom. "That man is poised to be a far more powerful player than you could ever be, with very powerful friends."

Merlin stood unmoved by the returned threat. "It's still early. Who knows what could make someone like that topple. But it's adorable how protective you are." He leaned in close to Cal with an intimate air. "Do you fancy this a date, Calvin? How sweet. But at the end of the night, you're still a *whore*. You might forget that, but he won't."

Cal didn't get hung up on that word. He knew what most people thought, no matter how comfortable he was in his own skin. He didn't *care* what other people thought of him. But as he glanced across the room to find Owen in the crowd, he knew there was one man's opinion he'd started to care about more than he should.

"Don't worry, I'll leave the boy alone," Merlin said, downing the last of his champagne. "He doesn't have to worry about *me*. Have a nice night."

The words lingered after Merlin walked away like smoke thick enough to choke on.

Cal moved back to Owen eventually but at a slow pace to gather his walls and not make it too obvious how much Merlin had shaken him. He must have failed, though, because Owen leaned over and whispered, "You okay?"

"Not a nice man," Cal whispered back, "but harmless. Forget him. I want you to enjoy tonight." He hoped he was right about Merlin, but now wasn't the time to worry.

Owen, for his part, nodded to appease Cal but betrayed a shadow of concern.

"So...." The taller of the couple Owen had been chatting with smiled. "Owen's publicist?"

The rest of the evening continued as if there hadn't been a single hiccup. Cal didn't spot Merlin in the crowd again, but he itched to whisk Owen away, fearing now more than ever that enemies waited in the wings.

There was more champagne and cocktails and food. Owen donated a respectable amount to the cause. They stuck close to Frank and Paul from then on, which was just as well. Eventually when things started to wind down, Cal and Owen snuck outside to find a cab without making a big deal over their departure.

Owen rested his head against Cal's shoulder during the ride back to his apartment. The night had taken its toll. Cal thrived off being the center of attention, but for Owen it was draining. And both of them had been drained by sinister men lately.

It was a relief to shed their glasses and their suits, to crawl into bed and snuggle like a normal, *real* couple. It wasn't real. It wasn't a date—it was Cal's *job*. But it plagued him how much he wished that could be different.

"Thank for you tonight," Owen said, though he'd thanked Cal plenty already.

"My pleasure, Owen. Any time."

"How long can you stay tomorrow?"

"How long do you want me?"

The pause made Cal wonder what Owen *wanted* to say. "We can get breakfast? Then I should do some work before lunch."

"Whatever you need."

Cal had taken Owen on as a client to help them both with their needs, but what he wanted now was getting harder to deny.

**OWEN** woke the next morning sluggish but content to find a familiar face in his bed and strong arms around him. When Cal blinked awake as well, blue eyes hypnotic and so kind, Owen recalled the question from last night.

*"How long do you want me?"*

It wounded him that he could never tell Cal the truth.

## Chapter Six

**DEPLOYING** the new police program felt like sending a child off to school for the first time. Owen was protective, nervous, and constantly checking in to make sure everything was going smoothly.

To some extent, it was out of his hands now. Models needed to take in live data to be adjusted, so nothing could be done until a few weeks went by with the boys in blue out in the field. Then, as real-world situations played out, his team could reevaluate and shift officer deployment accordingly, especially if crime went down in one area because more police were around, but then increased in others because the criminals changed course.

Which was what Owen expected to happen. It would be a constantly moving target that his models were built to adjust for automatically. Someone just needed to be paying attention to react.

There were a few protests around racial and class targeting the first week, which Wesley headed off by further explaining the training and equipment given out to ensure that didn't happen. If it ever started to look like any one group was being singled out, he would personally take responsibility for putting a stop to it. There was even a hotline for people to report abuses.

The initial calls were false alarms or pranks, but taking the extra precautions added credibility and accountability to the program. Things were looking good; the officers were doing their jobs. Now what mattered was if the program worked and overall crime started to decline.

Because of the program's release, Owen was that much busier in the weeks following the fundraiser with events and interviews, along with his side project between Nye Industries and Walker Tech. Sometimes he asked Cal to be his publicist date or to assist with actual publicist tasks, and sometimes they had quiet evenings in, but regardless of the nature of their time together, Owen kept adding more appointments for Cal's company, even if just to have him there when he got home at night.

The messages from Harrison had stopped, but every time Owen's phone chimed or he checked his email, he wondered when the eye of the hurricane would be over and the storm would start anew—one he couldn't sit back and enjoy, but that would shake him to his core like being struck by lightning.

The one benefit to it all was that his training with Lorelei had surpassed several more learning curves.

"Hey, Owen! Still on for this week?" Frank caught him in the hallway on his way to—actually, he had to stop and think if he was going to Walker Tech next, city hall, or just the bathroom. His life never seemed to slow down anymore.

"Of course!" Owen said, remembering he was having friends over for a game night, finally taking Frank up on his offer from when he first started this adventure. "I can't believe everyone agreed on Greek. I've been wanting to order from that place down the street from my apartment for weeks."

"Awesome!" Frank said. "Will Cal be there too?"

"Oh...." Owen clammed up, still caught off guard whenever someone asked about Cal, though of course they would when he rarely attended an event without the other man's presence. "I don't know if that would be... appropriate?"

The truth was, Owen wanted nothing more than to invite Cal, but it was different from a normal night in or a busy night out that fit into Cal's "services." It felt wrong to pay him for something that Owen ultimately only wanted him to attend if *he* wanted to be there.

Cal was a good friend, but the flow of money between them tainted the whole thing even though Owen knew it shouldn't. He shouldn't expect Cal to shun him if the business side of their relationship wasn't involved. Cal wasn't like that. And Owen would never take advantage or expect things from Cal should they become *just* friends someday.

But that was the problem. Where did the lines cross? What was acceptable and what wasn't when money played such an important role in their relationship? Owen could figure out complicated equations all day long, but that problem he hadn't solved yet.

"Because he's your publicist?" Frank asked with a waggled eyebrow. "Or because he's your Julia Roberts?"

Owen's eyes widened, mouth agape, unsure how to respond other than blurting, "How did you know that?"

"I'm a statistician," Frank said, not at all antagonistic. "I did the math. I'm the one who saw you with that business card, remember? Plus, I also remember him from the Nick of Time catalog. *Nice* choice. I won't say anything!" he added, no doubt reading the sheer terror on Owen's face. "It's cool. I told you I wouldn't judge about the escort thing, and I meant it. He's been *escorting* you. That's what they do. Anyone can tell you're not sleeping together. Not that there'd be anything wrong if you were! I mean, aside from *legally*...."

"I... really? It's that obvious?" Which was what Owen *wanted*. He didn't want people thinking he was sleeping with his publicist, taking advantage of him like a creepy executive, but at the same time, "*How* obvious, because—"

"You could cut the UST with a butter knife."

"UST?"

"Unresolved sexual tension," Frank rattled off as if that were common knowledge—maybe it was; Owen was never in the loop on these things. "If you *were* sleeping together, that would have been resolved weeks ago. You want it to, though, right? *Resolve*." He waggled an eyebrow again. "He means something to you, I can tell, and not just because he makes an amazing publicist and looks good in a suit. Maybe he *is* your *Pretty Woman*. Uhh.... Pretty Man? *American Gigolo*?"

"Stop," Owen interrupted before Frank could rattle off any more movie titles. "Things don't happen like that in real life." No matter how much Owen might want them to. "It's messy and complicated and *not* a movie plot. I need to stop relying on Cal to feel comfortable." Despite not having the will or desire to let him go.

"Relying on him?" Frank repeated with exaggerated disbelief. "You're kicking ass, Owen, or haven't you been paying attention? *You*. With Cal *and* when he's not around. He might have helped you get through a tough transition in your life, but you're doing fine. Maybe you honestly just *like* him. Would that be so terrible?"

If Cal didn't feel the same way, Owen couldn't imagine anything worse.

"Hey." Frank grabbed his shoulder as if just then realizing how shell-shocked he was. "I'm prying and causing the Owen.exe program to reboot. You wanna grab lunch and pretend I wasn't being invasive of your personal life? I feel like we need some boyfriends time."

"...what?" Owen took a moment to process that—Owen.exe reboot indeed.

"Yeah...," Frank said, drawing out the vowels. "That didn't translate as well as when women say 'girlfriends time,' did it? Bro time? There we go." He snapped his fingers. "Bro lunch, Owen?"

Owen chuckled helplessly. Frank had a knack for making him feel scrambled and then put back together in minutes. That's what he needed to do right now. Eat. "Bro lunch. Thanks, Frank. That sounds perfect. And it's okay to pry into my personal life sometimes. If I didn't have good friends who did that sort of thing, I probably wouldn't *have* a personal life," he joked—a little too seriously.

"Good. Not that last part, I mean...." Frank shook his head at his own foot-in-mouth syndrome. "I'm glad you see me as a friend. Come on. Let's go eat."

It had been easy to let things continue on their natural course with Cal, especially to further banish how Harrison made Owen feel. But something had to give soon, and Owen wasn't sure what that was. He just knew he liked having Cal around even when he didn't need him.

**CAL** sat at his computer desk by the window, staring at his calendar and just how much of it was taken up by *Scarlet*. That's what he'd wanted. That's what he *still* wanted. But what if he was holding Owen back from moving on with his life and truly healing?

There had always been the expectation that this was more temporary than Cal's other regulars, but whenever he thought Owen might call things off, another evening got booked.

Cal wasn't oblivious to being a stand-in for Owen's ex, a replacement that could fulfill needs Harrison had neglected. That didn't mean he wasn't valued in Owen's eyes as just *him*. He never worried about that; Owen wasn't *like* that. What Cal worried about was whether this was healthy or the absolute worst thing for Owen right now.

Maybe it was the worst thing for *him* too, given how often his thoughts strayed to Owen.

Claire's name blinked at him from his cell phone.

"Someone's been busy," he greeted.

"Look who's talking. You're allowed to initiate calls too, ya know."

"I've had a full schedule lately. How ya been, sis?"

"Thankful for Impulse. It's my new favorite spot. The drinks are to *die* for. Fantastic food too. If I'm five pounds heavier next time you're in town, it's all your fault."

Cal chuckled. He and his sister shared the same tricky metabolism of putting on and taking off weight at the drop of a hat, which might seem like a blessing on the losing side, but the gaining part could be annoying. In Cal's line of work, that meant constant upkeep.

"Did you meet the owner?" he asked, genuinely curious. "Usually works the bar?"

"Maybe. Cute blond guy? Or dark-skinned knockout?"

"Both technically. They're married."

"Well that's just unfair," Claire snorted. "Haven't been up at the bar as much as the dining area, but they seem nice. How do you know them?"

"I don't," Cal said, recognizing the hole he'd walked into. "Just heard about the place from a friend."

"Calvin, you don't have friends."

"I have—"

"Rhys and Lara, I know. Ever think of expanding?"

Cal had more friends than Rhys and Lara. Didn't he? Maybe he only had clients. Owen was a friend, but would they still be friends when their business relationship ended?

"Like I said, full schedule lately." He tried to dismiss the topic.

"Mmm," Claire hummed.

"What now? Think I sound listless again?"

"No. Now you sound conflicted, like you've found what your listlessness proved you were missing but don't know what to do with it. *Calvin,*" she said with sudden enthusiasm, "did you meet your Richard Gere and not tell me?"

"Why does my line of work always come with *Pretty Woman* correlations?" he groaned.

"Gee, I can't imagine."

"He's not some savior I need to rescue me from my life. I love my life."

"Yet you just admitted there's a specific *he.*"

*Crap.*

"*Calvin.* You fell in love with a client!"

"I'm not in lo—"

"And it's got you freaking out because you figure he'll only see your worth in dollar signs."

Cal's stomach dropped. He wasn't *in love* with Owen. That was juvenile, ridiculous. He just… enjoyed Owen's company more than anyone else's.

"He's not like that," he said, rather than deny Claire's accusations. Owen didn't see Cal's worth in any bottom line, but money was still part of the problem, because it permeated every interaction they'd ever had. Changing the nature of their relationship now would throw things off, make seeing each other awkward in ways Cal couldn't stomach. It was easier to leave things be.

"Then what *is* he like?" Claire asked without the tease. "Tell me."

Maybe Cal had been avoiding initiating calls to his sister because he knew this would come up, and he hadn't been ready to share Owen with her yet. It was different with Rhys. They always talked shop and exchanged client stories, but that had dwindled lately too, from both of them. Telling Claire about his work was distasteful anyway, but this wasn't pillow talk—this was *Owen*.

Cal found it surprisingly easy to describe the young man and reminisce about the evenings they'd spent together, not hiding that sex wasn't part of the workload. It was companionship. Support. Not *love*. Cal wasn't in love. Love was too dangerous.

"You broke rule number one, Cal. You're dating a client."

"We're not dating."

"He may be paying you, but what you're doing is *dating*. Just without the fun bits at the end of the night." She snickered.

The weird thing was, Cal didn't miss the "fun bits" when he was with Owen. He thought about them, craved the kid in ways that *ached*, but their talks and dinners, their nights spent listening to Sinatra or surfing sci-fi movies on Netflix, were more fulfilling than the short-lived pleasures his other clients gave him.

Cal wished he could have *both*, but he didn't think that existed for him.

"He's had it rough, Claire. He needs something… more than me."

"Calvin," she said with a touch of sadness. "What if, for once, just once, you realized *you* could be enough for someone? At least give this guy the benefit of the doubt. I've never heard you talk about someone like you describe him. He sounds perfect for you. The same boring old man deep down and a giant dork."

Cal glared at his reflection in the nearby window. "Thanks for that."

Claire giggled. "In reality, he does sound young, but I won't judge a little cradle robbing if he makes you happy."

Glancing at the clock on his computer screen, Cal realized that if he didn't start getting ready, he'd be late. He was never late with clients. "I have to go. My work day starts when yours ends, remember?"

"Fine. But if you're seeing *him* tonight, maybe suck it up and go after what you really want. You know I've never looked down on your profession." She turned serious again. "People can do whatever they want with their bodies as long as they enjoy themselves. If they can make money on it too, well, more power to 'em. But if what you want changes, you are allowed to pursue something new, even if it's terrifying.

"I thought you were a gambling man, big brother. It's not a gamble if it isn't a risk."

Cal had said that phrase to her countless times, usually when she doubted herself before making a big decision. She always rolled her eyes at him, even if ultimately, she thanked him for the push.

He wasn't sure if he was as brave as her in the end, but her words followed him that night all the way to a familiar apartment door.

When the young, bespectacled brunet answered his knock, Cal poured all of his desire and frustration into a desperate lunge forward, claiming pliant lips before any words could be spoken. Grasping hands twisted into his shirt, a surprised mouth opening after the initial shock with pleased whimpers, their tongues sliding past each other smooth and wet.

This was what Cal wanted. *Touch* that connected deeper than skin contact, enough to feel the warm body against him heat up further the longer they kissed and writhed in time to the shudders pulsing between them. It was exhilarating, *electric*, and *so* good.

Cal just wished the lips he was kissing were *Owen's*.

"Someone's eager," Piper husked like a roughened purr. He was shorter than Owen by almost half a foot, eyes brown and body more filled out than Owen's slender frame, but there were similarities that made it easy to pretend. "I like it."

"I missed you," Cal said, grazing his teeth along Piper's jaw and kicking the door closed behind him as he pawed at his prey just the way he knew Piper liked it. "Can't wait to get my *mouth* on you."

"Ooo, *yes*, Daddy. Get me on the bed."

Only the faint twitch of Cal's smile betrayed his distaste for the endearment. It was the one thing that irked him about Piper, but he was easy to make vocal in other ways and was one of Cal's favorite clients. The fact that the things he liked best about him overlapped with what he liked about *Owen* was beside the point.

His energy, his floof of brunet hair, his love of music and *good* art. He wasn't sweet or timid like Owen, but the similarly pale skin could almost make Cal forget who he was with.

Piper was easy to lift and carry toward the bedroom, legs wrapping around Cal's waist as the contented noises he made were licked from his mouth. They had a very specific arrangement, where Cal saw him before every concert to help him relax. He'd give Piper his *full* attention—usually on his knees—then give *himself* attention while Piper got dressed.

Tonight, like many before it, Cal had been hired to wait in Piper's bed until the concert ended. Piper swore it helped him play better, having Cal's mouth on him beforehand, knowing throughout the entire concert he was waiting back at the apartment for round two.

Cal enjoyed this arrangement as much as he enjoyed all his regulars and their various desires. He'd thrived off of how appreciative Piper in particular could be for almost two years. The last thing Cal should have wished for was that the noises Piper was making were Owen's.

He shouldn't have imagined slenderer thighs when he kissed his way up them. Shouldn't have envisioned longer fingers clawing at the sheets. Shouldn't have closed his eyes and felt his way through every attention he lavished on his partner, conjuring hazel green looking back at him and a dimpled smile. But all of that spurred him on and made it easier to be there when part of him was elsewhere.

"*Wow*," Piper exhaled when it was over. "You outdid yourself. Maybe you really did miss me."

"Always," Cal said, playing his role to perfection as he pressed his lips to the inside of Piper's thigh.

The rest happened like clockwork—a bruising kiss before Piper went to shower, Cal stroking himself until he returned, then putting on a show while Piper looked on and slipped into his tuxedo. Even then, Cal imagined a different suit on the young man watching him—in *burgundy*.

Later, left to clean up, Cal had the run of the apartment. He donned the robe that had been set out for him, downed a glass of water, then poured himself a stronger drink while he played Billie Holiday from the impressive sound system. He had hours before Piper would be back. Master of his domain, when he'd arrived, now, and later when Piper returned, *this* was the sort of evening Cal lived for.

Once.

He couldn't help comparing views when he went to the window, because this was better than his own apartment's outlook on the city, but it didn't hold a candle to Owen's.

Claire was right, it was *terrifying* how much more Cal wanted from life, because he didn't think it was a gamble he could take.


**OWEN** should go to bed. His eyes were sore from staring at computer screens all day, and the last thing he needed was to stare at his TV until all hours of the night. Not that it was terribly late. He just didn't want to go to bed early even if he was tired. He tended to stall going to bed on nights when Cal wasn't with him, because the thought of getting under those covers alone sunk his heart like a stone in a pond.

He didn't do well alone.

He'd been doing well *across the board*, apparently, but he didn't feel that way.

Pausing in his Netflix queue on one of the more recent Japan-made *Godzilla* movies, Owen was about to press Play when he stopped himself. Cal would *love* this movie; he didn't want to watch it without him.

Snagging his phone from the coffee table, Owen looked at the time again to be sure it wasn't too late and dialed his sister in a last-ditch effort for sanity.

"Are you finally ready to tell me whatever secret you and Casey have been keeping behind my back?"

"I don't even get a 'hello?'" Owen deflected, despite being the one who'd called her, "or 'how are you, brother dear, I love you and miss your face'?"

"Cute, O," Alyssa droned, "but *no*, not when you've been conspiring with my husband."

"It's not conspiring, just... *avoiding*." He was surprised she hadn't pestered him sooner.

"Owen." Her voice dropped to a more sympathetic pitch. "What did you do?"

Staring at the Netflix screen, Owen sighed at the cliché picture he painted, just like having ice cream for dinner. "I took your advice. And I think I might hate you for it."

The truth poured out of him easier than he expected, maybe because Alyssa stayed silent while he explained how he'd hired an escort that first week in Atlas City and had been scheduling him regularly since. He told her about every late night, every event, every snuggle on the sofa or in bed, and how hard it was not to push for more when every moment with Cal was the best part of his day sometimes.

"When I said you could hire an escort to make things easier, I didn't think you'd fall for the guy."

"I didn't—"

"*Owen.*"

She knew how hard he fell when he liked someone. He'd fallen hard for Harrison once—hard enough to give his whole self over to a man who took him for granted. Cal would never do that. Owen trusted *Cal*. It was himself he didn't trust, not to find some way to screw this up, especially if it was….

"…real?"

"Huh?" Owen said, more distracted than he'd realized.

"What I said was is this something you need to put a stop to before you get in too deep… or is it real?"

"It couldn't be real. I pay him."

"Okay, but if money wasn't involved, how would you feel then?"

Owen knew the answer, but he was experienced in rejection, even if it had been years since he'd been single. He could picture clearly the pitying look Cal would give him when he turned him down, as gently as possible of course, which would almost be worse than being laughed at. Cal wouldn't laugh. He was too nice for that, too good at his job, but he'd still turn Owen down. People probably fell in love with him all the time.

"Think about it," Alyssa said. "If this is hurting you more than helping, maybe it's time to end it. But if it is something real, don't doubt yourself so much, okay? And next time," she added with a touch of sass, "don't get Casey to lie for you. You know he's terrible at that."

"Sorry." Owen laughed. "And thanks, Lyssa. Really." She was probably right anyway—about the first part. He should cut his losses before things got awkward, before it got too difficult to let Cal go. It wasn't real. It couldn't be real.

But after the call, Owen decided to wait on the *Godzilla* movie, just in case.

**"MR.** Mercer?"

"Hmm?"

Cal focused on Dick behind the desk, reminding himself that he was in the office, in midconversation, and could not afford to daydream.

Dick fixed him with a calculating stare. "As I said, perhaps you could pick up some basic escort assignments if you're weary and needing a break, though I understand you prefer *complete package* clients."

Right. Dick had finally pressed Cal about not filling the empty slot for Narcissus. Cal didn't want to add a new regular. He'd even been debating who else he could cut to lighten his load more for... shit, *Owen*. What the hell was he doing?

"Mr. Mercer?"

"I'm listening." Cal struggled not to snap.

"Your schedule is your own," Dick said. "You're certainly still pulling your weight financially. I merely wished to express my curiosity and ensure nothing was out of sorts."

"I'm fine, just tired. Maybe I will take on some simpler escort requests for a while."

"Certainly. That option is always available. Mr. Kane appears to be lightening his load as well." Dick shifted from concern to thinly veiled suspicion, tapping his desk as his attention diverted to the aggregate calendar on his computer. "You don't have any insight there, do you?"

"Why don't you ask Rhys himself?"

"That tends to prove... ineffectual."

Cal snorted, which turned into clearing his throat. "Sorry, Dick. No idea what might be going on."

"Naturally," Dick sighed. "Was there anything else?"

Nothing he could help with, just that Cal was *drowning,* and the only way to save him was to let him sink or make a daring rescue—by dropping Owen altogether.

Merlin had been right about one thing: Owen would want someone untainted when he was finally ready to stop paying for company. It would be worse if Owen clung to Cal because of the trauma he'd escaped and the struggles he still faced. Maybe it was time for Cal to remove the temptation from both of them and fill his schedule with new regulars. Or maybe every option he'd been juggling was wrong, and he needed a vacation.

Even escorts needed vacation sometimes. Cal had never taken one, but he found himself opening his mouth—

A raised voice echoed down the hallway, drawing their attention to the door. Lara darted past as if she'd already been alerted to the commotion before things escalated loud enough to reach them. Casting a brief glance back at Dick, Cal raced out of the office to follow her as Dick gave chase behind him.

By the time they reached the front, Daphne was on her feet, talking animatedly with security over the phone, while Lara had a man with shorn platinum hair pressed to the wall with his arm twisted up behind his back. Being a half head taller than the petite woman in no way gave the man an advantage, which he'd obviously already learned.

"Are you aware who you're manhandling, Miss Tyler?" he seethed against the wall.

"Everyone looks the same to me, Mr. Compton," Lara said, while her hold remained secure and her words bit out close and sharp at his ear, "either worth my time or not. Guess where you fall at the moment?"

"I'm a *client*," he growled, as if that excused his bad behavior. "And I'm dissatisfied. I demand—"

"Why don't you take a nap until security arrives?" Lara said, and in one sure move, she pressed her forearm to his windpipe until he passed out, where she released him, checked his pulse, and left him on the floor.

Dick straightened his suit with a nod at Daphne, who'd just finished alerting security. "Everything all right, Miss Tyler?" he turned to her.

With a crack of her wrists, Lara smiled. "Perfectly under control, sir."

It wasn't the first time Cal had seen Lara deal with an unruly client who'd made their way to the office to cause trouble. Cal didn't even know who this man was serviced by—*formerly* serviced by, clearly. Certainly formerly now.

The point was, he wasn't shaken by the confrontation or violence. What shook him was that the only thing he could think about while staring at the unconscious man at Lara's feet wasn't him or even Merlin, but *Harrison Marsh* and what little worth that man had attributed to Owen.

The emails had dwindled, but Cal knew men like Harrison. He was looking at one right now. He didn't want to leave Owen in the lurch, but he didn't want to be a crutch for him either. He... he was all turned around, unable to form a plan that made sense, when he was always, *always* in control. Owen made him feel like he was free-falling, and he couldn't understand why he liked that so much.

"Calvin?" Lara asked, gripping his arm to drag him back down to earth.

"Keep my schedule clear tonight," he said, and turned on his heel to head out the door.

"Mr. Mercer!" Dick called after him, but Cal was already gone.

He wasn't scheduled to see Owen tonight, but he had no other appointments, and he needed to sort through this, needed to find out where they stood, untwist what he and Owen were to each other so he could make a clean break if that's what was needed. If Owen had grown too reliant on him, he should break things off anyway.

That's what he expected to find when he ended up outside Owen's door—a broken man, desperate as always to see him. But as soon as Cal finished knocking, dressed more casually than usual in a simple black sweater and jeans, he realized that the sounds coming from inside the apartment were not that of a lone man watching TV.

Owen had company. What the hell was Cal doing here?

Backing up, seconds from bolting, Cal was blasted with an increase in volume of group *laughter* when the door opened and Owen's smiling face confronted him.

"Cal!" Owen exclaimed before his smile fell in lieu of *guilt*. "Oh no, did I forget I had you scheduled tonight?"

"No, I…." Cal jumped in to soften Owen's rambling. "You didn't. We didn't. I shouldn't… be here. You have friends over." He could see Frank and Paul over Owen's shoulder and another couple he couldn't quite make out.

"Well, yeah, but… *you're* a friend." Owen renewed his smile with a shy glance at the floor. "You should come in. I wanted to invite you, but I wasn't sure if that would be… weird?"

"Who is it, Owen?" Frank called from inside, though he could clearly see Cal. He was grinning, though, so Cal didn't think the man was being facetious to be rude.

Owen was doing well even without Cal's presence, settling in fine and making new friends. That was…

good. That's what Cal had hoped to find even if he didn't expect it because it meant he wasn't holding Owen back.

But then… maybe Owen didn't need him anymore.

"It's Cal!" Owen said before seizing Cal's hand to pull him inside. "Come on. It's okay. Please?" He gave Cal this private little smile, squeezing his hand until Cal had to smile back and go along with him to please the pounding of his pulse. "You remember Frank and Paul."

Cal was summarily dragged to the living room where the couple sat on one section of Owen's large L-shaped sofa, and the other couple—

"*Lorelei*," Cal stuttered to a stop, recognizing the young woman as soon as he saw her face.

As floored as Cal was to see her there, she seemed entirely unfazed to see him. "Good to see you again, Calvin."

"You know my trainer?" Owen said. *Of course*—his self-defense trainer. Cal should have guessed it was the same Lorelei, but he'd never known her profession. "How do you two know each… uhh…." He trailed off as his mind supplied the *wrong* conclusion.

"No, we—"

"Cal works with my sister." Lorelei saved him. "Lara."

"Oh," Owen said in painfully obvious relief. Then his eyes widened. "*Lara Tyler*?"

"Tyler is my maiden name," Lorelei said.

Cal's eyes drifted over the group, to Lorelei who *knew*, to her husband who obviously knew as well now that Lara had been mentioned, and with the way Frank wore an amused, bitten-back smile and his husband looked on like this was all too fascinating not to stare at, it became glaringly clear that everyone in the room knew Cal *wasn't* Owen's publicist.

"I should go." He turned for the door.

"What? *Why?*" Owen clutched after him, gripping his wrist tightly for a moment, only to let his fingers retract in apology. He moved close to Cal anyway, eager and uncertain but not as small as the man Cal had first met. "You don't have to leave. It's just Trivial Pursuit. You can stay if you want to."

Didn't Owen understand they all knew what he was? Maybe he didn't. Maybe he was too naïve to get it. But the flush to his cheeks seemed to say otherwise, and he simply didn't care.

"Are you sure *you* want me to?" Cal asked.

Owen looked effervescent tonight, relaxed in one of his newer, nicer pairs of jeans but with a *Star Wars* T-shirt and zip-up sweater. "Why wouldn't I?" he said, too sincere, too *good*. "It's an evening for friends. As long as you want to be here, I... want that too."

This was not what Cal had come here for, but then he didn't know *what* he'd come here for. Answers. Direction. Absolution maybe. Owen's smile held all those things.

"Okay. I'll stay." In a rush, all the tension drained from Cal's shoulders just by making Owen look that happy. He let Owen take his coat, then sat with him on the sofa beside Lorelei and, "Tommy, was it?"

"Nice to see you again," he said. They'd met briefly through Lara.

"You too."

There wasn't judgment in anyone's eyes, least of all in Frank's, despite the man's dopey grin—Cal saw that now.

"It's actually *Lord of the Rings* Trivial Pursuit," Frank said.

Glancing at the board on the coffee table, Cal asked, "Books or movies?"

"Both," Paul said excitedly.

"Well in that case—" Cal chuckled, meeting Owen's gaze from where he sat close enough at Cal's side for their hips to touch. "—none of you stand a chance."

**IT** felt like their first night all over again. Tentative and thrilling and so much *fun*. The only difference this time was that Owen got to share how wonderful Cal was with other people, and so differently than at some stiff social event. Cal also *crushed* it on the Tolkien lore, which made him even more perfect, something Owen never would have thought possible.

Not once did Owen think about schedules or the other clients Cal saw, at least not until everyone else was getting ready to leave, abandoning him to Cal's company after a completely not-date *date*.

Then it was definitely like their first night, because how did Owen proceed from point A to point B without making a fool of himself? The topic of *money* when nothing had been scheduled beforehand loomed over them like a storm cloud. It had been easy to push that aside while playing games and eating and enjoying drinks with the other couples. The other couples—as if *they* were a couple.

Lorelei and Tommy left first, followed immediately by Frank and Paul. It did not help that Frank winked at Owen on his way out either.

"Small world," Cal said from the kitchen, having brought glasses to the sink to help clean up. "Or maybe it's just this city."

"Y-yeah." Owen scratched the back of his head as he moved toward Cal. "Maybe I can meet Lara sometime." *Or was that weird? Was Owen making things weird?*

"Maybe…," Cal said, too cryptic to read, like even he wasn't sure if he meant that. Turning to lean against the cabinets, he faced Owen like another familiar picture from their past, yet everything was different tonight, paved in uneven ground neither knew how to tread. "I should head home too. Unless…."

"Unless?" Owen perked up.

"Unless…." Cal gestured at Owen like *he* was the summed-up answer.

Because Owen was the client. Because Owen set the rules. Being handed back the reins didn't make him feel very in control right now. "Oh. You don't *have* to stay and snuggle or anything. We can say it was just between friends tonight. Unless you *want* to be paid!" Oh God, now Owen felt like a complete *goon*.

Cal didn't look upset, though. He laughed lightly like Owen had surprised him. "This can be unpaid, Owen. It was a night off for me."

His night *off*? "But I still made you work."

"It didn't feel like work." Cal took a breath as if more words waited on his tongue, as if he wanted to say, *you never feel like work.*

The blush filling Owen's cheeks made him certain his hair was about to catch fire. He was reading into things. Cal was just being nice. Cal had… come here on his night *off.* "Oh! I forgot to ask! Why did you come over if you weren't scheduled? Did you need to talk to me about something?"

For the first time since Owen had known Cal, the other man looked unsure how to answer. Then the apprehension melted from his expression and he just looked at Owen, content and unguarded—not an act, not a role, just.... Cal.

"You know, I can't remember. Guess I just wanted to see you."

Not knowing how to compute that, Owen erupted in surprised laughter. Cal wanted to see him. Cal didn't care about the business side. He just wanted to *see him*. "Cool! *Good*. You can always come see me if you want to. Tonight was really fun."

What came next, however, was shrouded in mystery. Owen didn't want to ruin the magic by *speaking* again. He hoped Cal would take the initiative, and as it turned out, he did—by heading for the door. Which was *fine*, definitely the right call, but Owen felt like he was flailing following at his heels.

It was the first time they hadn't ended an evening in their underwear, creating such a unique dynamic that was somehow more intimate with clothes on. All Owen could think about as he accompanied Cal to the door was that he wished he could kiss him goodbye, but then he'd be taking advantage of the offer of just a night between *friends*.

Still, there was hope now like a buzz of electricity between them that was better than any brush of skin.

"Good night." Owen gripped the edge of his door for balance, not ready to shut it behind Cal just yet.

Cal hesitated, nodded like he'd convinced himself to complete some insurmountable act, then leaned forward to press a soft kiss to Owen's cheek. "Good night, Owen."


**OWEN** hummed when he was happy. He'd been told it was highly annoying.

But he couldn't help it! He'd slept *great* last night and had carried a skip in his step since the moment he walked out the door. Today, he was at Walker Tech again, head down working on data sets that would eventually need reviewing from multiple departments as well as Nye Industries. It was the perfect sort of workday for him, because he could live in his own world for a while and just get things done. He needed days like that.

Especially when his head was wrapped in a fluffy cloud of *Cal.* And that kiss. And their perfect night.

Owen still had Cal scheduled for several events and evenings coming up, but everything was different now, and even knowing that the conversation of "what do we do next?" still lay ahead, Owen felt confident in the outcome. He felt giddy.

He'd been listening to DragonForce and Lordi on his headphones all day—not *Lorde*, which had confused Alyssa the first time he mentioned the band and played her one of their songs. "Let's Go Slaughter He-Man" was not the same genre as "Royals." But with metal blaring in his ears, he was in the *zone*, even when just refilling his coffee or grabbing a snack. He'd have his work done in half the time at this rate.

Sure, a few people in the break room or hallways snickered at him or seemed to be whispering about something with glances his direction—probably because he was still an antisocial dork most of the time; what else could they be whispering about—but he didn't care. He was on top of the world right now.

"Hey, Owen, can I steal you for a minute?"

Until Adam waved a hand in front of his face and Owen had to tug out his earbuds. "Hi! Sorry. And yeah, of course, what's up?"

"Good news. Always good news. Come on." Adam pulled Owen along with him and kept a firm hold for the first few steps toward the conference rooms. He was one of those overly physical people, but Owen didn't mind so much now that he knew Adam.

"I like good news," Owen said. "About the project?"

"Yep! We have another interested partner that could really help this blow up."

"Really? Who?"

"Orion Labs in Middleton."

Owen stumbled over his feet, which he wished he could blame on keeping up with Adam's pace. "That's… great. They're a good company. Lots of resources."

"Exactly. Some of their people contacted us after that press release about the new venture. They'd like to get in on things too, maybe offer some support and additional scientists to help see this through. Apparently one of their top brass worked with you before and really knows your models?"

"Uhh… well…."

"I figured it was the least I could do to hear out his proposal in person."

"What?" Owen's heart pounded in his ears louder than the drums had been pulsing over his headphones. "You…. *H-he's*…."

Adam led Owen into the main conference room with a flourish where a tall, trim, striking man in his early forties stood waiting with the most satisfied, snakelike grin.

*Harrison.*

"Hello, Owen."

# Chapter Seven

**OWEN'S** vision tunneled, zeroing in on the face, the figure, the *man* he hadn't laid eyes on in months. Rooted to the spot just inside the conference room door, he couldn't move until Adam snapped him back to consciousness with a pat on the back.

"Owen, Harrison tells me you two know each other pretty well."

How *dare* he? He wasn't merely grinning like a snake, he *was* one—a viper waiting to strike.

"We worked parallel to each other for years," Harrison said, crossing the room to approach them with measured steps. "So we didn't often cross paths, but I know his work well. Owen was always exceptional."

*Snake.*

"No surprise there. I'm just lucky to get some of his divided attention." Adam laughed, and Owen knew he should react, speak, *scream*, but he couldn't move. He'd been thrown back in time almost half a year, and he had no idea how to respond.

Even Harrison's glasses were the same—black on top but clear along the bottom. Owen remembered when he got them. Today he wore a blue patterned suit, one of Owen's favorites because of how it complemented his eyes, with a crisp shirt and tie.

The one difference was his hair, cut shorter on the sides to look more modern, more fitting for Atlas City, like he planned to stick around.

"You're staying for the presentation, right?" Owen turned to Adam without acknowledging Harrison directly.

"Of course. You can't do all the heavy lifting." Adam patted his back again, hovering close like Owen usually found intrusive, but today he was grateful. "Just one second, I want to grab a few of the gang from R&D. Plus, I figured you'd want a couple minutes to catch up. I'll be right back."

Owen tried, he really did, to say something—no, wait, *stop*—but the air crystalized in his lungs and seared him with every breath he choked on until Adam was out the door, abandoning him in a secluded room with his—

*Not* ex. Harrison didn't deserve to be called just an "ex" when Lorelei had worked so hard to get him to admit what the man really was.

A user. An *abuser*. A snake, a rotten snake, he was a—

"Owen?"

Breath catching just as fiercely when his eyes landed on Harrison again, Owen saw that confident façade drop away, leaving the older man looking… scared. And *sorrowful*. And like every other time he'd convinced Owen to stay with him.

*Channel it,* Owen thought as he remembered the lies that followed. *Use it. Be angry—you have a* right *to be angry.*

"Hear me out." Harrison raised his hands.

"*No,*" Owen spat with more bite than he expected. Focusing on that small win, he clenched his fists tighter. "What are you doing here, Harry? Are you out of your mind? Adam doesn't know our history, but if you think I won't tell him the truth—"

"I'm not here to cause trouble."

"Even *worse* if you think you can win me back—"

"I'm not here for that either." He came closer, too close, keeping the large table and the rest of the conference room behind him since Owen hadn't moved from the door. "I understand if you can never forgive me for that night. I took you for granted, for years. I know that now. I'm here because I honestly believe this business decision is a sound one, but I could have sent someone else to make the proposal. The truth is, I wanted the chance to tell you how sorry I am."

*Lies.* It was a lie. It was *always* a lie. "I didn't answer your emails because I *don't* want to talk to you. How did you even get—"

"If you want to tell Walker our history and that it's unprofessional for me to be here, I'll bow out."

"It *is* unprofessional," Owen barked back. "It was unprofessional for you to get your *boyfriend* a job so you could watch me all day and steal my work."

"Steal?" Harrison reared back like he had no idea what Owen was talking about.

No. *No*. He did not get to do this again. "You stole every idea I ever had. You *won't* steal this."

"Owen." Harrison raised his hands once more as if to appease him, as if Owen was the unreasonable one. "I asked if it was okay every time I presented your ideas. You just needed one more promotion to get on the radar of the other execs, then they would have listened without me. I told you that."

"You could have let me present my ideas myself and backed me instead."

"For them to find out we were sleeping together, *living* together, and assume that was the only reason I was vouching for you?" His words came out so sincere, so rational, that Owen floundered for how to counter him. "Yes, I used your research, but I always asked. I never demanded. I never stole anything."

That… wasn't true, was it?

He *had* asked, if Owen thought about it, and Owen always agreed… but only because he felt like he had no other choice! Harrison had manipulated him. This was all part of the game. *This* was how he'd controlled Owen for years.

"I'm not having this argument." Owen shut him down; he had to shut him *down*.

But Harrison reached for him—

"Owen—"

—for his *arm*, and Owen couldn't, he *couldn't*. He staggered back, knocking into the door in his haste to get away and hating how he trembled at the mere thought of Harrison's hands on him.

Harrison didn't pursue him but stopped midstep, arm outstretched, expression distressed and so mournful again. "Please. Don't flinch like that. You know I'd never hurt you."

"Never—" Rage boiled inside of Owen where fear had just bubbled. How could he say that? How could he *say that*? "You broke my *arm*."

"I… what?" His own arm dropped as he leaned away from Owen and the color drained from his face. "It was broken? You never told me that. I had no idea. You wouldn't even talk to me."

"Why should I have?" Owen stayed on the defensive, though he had to wonder if Harrison hadn't known. Not that it *mattered*. He'd still done it. Wasn't it worse if he hadn't noticed how rough he was being? "Why should I listen to you now? The only thing that's different is I'm happy and doing better without you."

It was everything Owen had rehearsed in his head, everything he'd longed to say but assumed he'd never get the chance. It didn't feel as vindicating as he'd envisioned, because Harrison was supposed to sneer at him and put him down, not shrink in on himself like he cared, like he was *sorry*.

"Were you never happy with me?" he asked in a small voice. "Never?"

Getting his trembling under control, Owen moved from the door, not closer to Harrison but parallel around him so he no longer felt trapped. "For a while I was," he said, because he had been, hadn't he? There were reasons he'd fallen for Harrison, valid reasons he'd wanted to be with him—once. "But not for a long time."

"Then I'm sorry for that too," Harrison said, eyes closing briefly before they opened, clouded and damp—which wasn't fair. It wasn't *fair*. He had no *right* to make this harder. "I'm not asking for a second chance. I'm asking for you to let me prove I can still be the man you once trusted and cared for so that maybe we can walk away from this without hating each other. That's all I'm after. Your forgiveness, only if you believe I deserve it, not your love. I know I lost that a long time ago.

"Walker will listen to whatever you want." He gestured at the door. "You're the one in demand here. You're the one everyone wants to please. So, if there is a second that passes where you want me or even all of Orion Labs out of the picture, just say the word and I'm gone. Your call. I won't fight what you want, even if that includes me leaving."

The *bastard* was taking the high road when all Owen wanted was to hate him. He'd finally gotten to a place where he felt justified in hating him, where he recognized what had been done to him all those years, how much he'd been used, how... awful....

But looking at Harry now, he saw some of the man he remembered from when they first met, and that made everything worse.

The door opened with a whoosh as Adam returned, followed by three members of the R&D team. "Okay!" He clapped. "Shall we get started? What are you doing back there, Owen?" He turned to peer at where Owen stood half-hidden behind the door.

"Nothing." Owen pulled on a smile and moved to grab a water bottle from the conference room minifridge. "Just getting a drink. Anyone else need something?"

He couldn't make a scene, *wouldn't* make a big deal of this. He just had to sit through the proposal and take his time deciding the best course of action. It would have been so much easier if Harrison had given him a reason to have him dragged out by security.

Throughout the presentation, Owen thought he'd be lost in a daze, unable to listen, but Harrison was good at pitching, a good storyteller, quick with a joke and warm smile, and always intuitive to when it was time to get serious. Orion Labs had more overseas contacts than Walker Tech or Nye Industries, more access to certain technologies that would keep production costs down. Anyone could tell that the proposal was mutually beneficial.

It was almost nice a few minutes here and there when Harry would have the room laughing along with him—*Owen* included—reminding him of the passionate, fiercely intelligent man Owen once found so enthralling. He wasn't an innovator. He didn't come up with new models or technologies the way Owen did, but he was good at implementation and bringing a project together.

"Well, if everyone's in agreement," Adam said, "I'll send the proposal to Ms. Nye for her take, maybe set something up for later this week, make sure our partner doesn't bite my head off for talking to you first." He chuckled, but Owen knew how scary Keri could be when given a reason. Adam turned to him last for his approval, for his say, and there was nothing Owen could do but nod.

When the others left, he stayed in the conference room with Harrison, even though part of him wanted to flee.

"You didn't say anything," Harrison said, quietly despite it only being the two of them.

"I wasn't going to tell a room full of my peers that you're an *asshole* and look like an asshole myself," Owen said. "It makes sense to collaborate with Orion Labs. It's a good proposal. You were always good at that sort of thing."

"I can ask for a representative to replace me, have someone else—"

"You're CTO," Owen cut him off, because this was hard enough without Harrison's sympathy. "It should be you. It's fine. I'm not going to be petty. But my decision doesn't mean *anything* else." Forcing himself to meet Harrison's eyes, he fought the instinctive shiver they stirred in him. "I don't want to see you. I don't want to talk to you. This is *just* professional."

"Of course." Harrison nodded without a single word of argument.

Moving swiftly to leave the room before anything else could be said, Owen hated more than anything else that *this* version of Harry… reminded him of the man he'd fallen in love with.


**"WHY** are you buying me a drink in the middle of the day?" Cal eyed Lara with suspicion.

Lara didn't take days off any more than he did, but there she was, treating him to a late lunch and a drink at their favorite dive bar. She looked different with her hair down, in a casual outfit and leather jacket, like she could bench press a bouncer and then slam a few shots. She ordered some too, along with a couple beers as if to prove the point.

"I have news," she said, "and trust me, after you hear it, you're gonna need a drink."

They clinked glasses and downed their shots, then took their beers from the bar to a corner table before she elaborated.

"The Godfather will no longer be using your services."

"That's it?" Cal hadn't been expecting the news, but he wasn't devastated by it. "Don't tell me *she* had an ex to go back to? I'll get a complex."

"Nope." Lara's blonde waves bounced as she shook her head. "Her father? Godfather *Senior*? Was just arrested for racketeering."

Cal gaped at her as she took a liberal drink from her beer. "You're joking."

"Aptly chosen code name, Calvin." She held her glass out for a toast.

He was too stunned to mirror her. "How did they catch him?"

"You have *Scarlet* to thank for that."

"The police program?"

"Extra officers were in the right place at the right time and caught Asher Morris," she whispered to keep his name private, "red-handed in the middle of offering protection to a local business. The news is going to be rampant with this for weeks, making your little data scientist look very good. You're seeing him later, right?"

This was amazing, everything Owen had hoped for, and it had inadvertently cleared more of Cal's schedule. Cal wished The Godfather all the best, she was a good kid, but he understood if her focus needed to be elsewhere.

Owen was going to be buzzing with elation tonight.

"I think this might call for a celebration when I head over." Finally Cal raised his glass to join Lara's toast and took a solid swig.

He wouldn't have another. He wanted to save his senses for Owen, especially since tonight was the perfect occasion to bring over an imported beer he'd been saving that would go well with what they planned to make for dinner.

"Now you only have Piper and Prince to pawn off and you can make a clean getaway." Lara eyed him over the rim of her mug.

Cal glowered. He should have known she'd start fishing if she was picking up the tab. "And why would I want to do that?"

"You know my sister called me last night, right?"

*Of course she did.* "I know how nosy sisters can be. Care to keep *your* nose out of my business?"

"Not if you're going to start having dinner parties with my family members." Lara downed almost all her remaining beer in one gulp, then smacked her lips when she slammed it down. "Lorelei had quite a few things to say about you two."

"Doesn't *Lorelei* have any sense of patient confidentiality?"

"She's a personal trainer."

"Who doubles as a therapist by Scarlet's description."

Lara pursed her lips to concede the point. "She didn't give any specifics, so *Scarlet's* secrets are safe, but in her words, you seemed like an entirely different man than the one she remembered meeting."

"That's what I do, Lara"—Cal spread his arms to encompass himself—"become the man my clients need me to be."

"Only you weren't on the clock last night."

*Dammit.* She had him, as easily as she could have hooked him into a headlock. "Look, if you're concerned about my work ethic—"

"I'm not here as your handler, Calvin." She dropped the sly smile. "I'm here as your friend. We've worked together a long time. I know how you handle clients. I know what normal looks like for you. And Lorelei's right. Lately you've been a different man, and anyone with eyes could see that it's because of *Owen Quinn*." Her voice dropped just as softly as it had when she said Morris, but Cal still tensed to hear Owen mentioned anywhere other than between them and their circle of public events.

He was supposed to be a master of personas, playing the right role to fit the right situation, even when that meant pulling on a mask to fool his friends, but Lara wasn't someone he could con. Lorelei wasn't either, apparently, not that Cal had tried conning anyone last night.

"It might not even matter," he said. "Maybe he doesn't think of me like—"

"Please," Lara interrupted. "Excuses don't become you. You can't do this forever. Even a man aging as gracefully as you are can't turn tricks in his sixties."

Cal frowned. A jab at his age was always a sore spot, because it *had* been grating on him lately, that sense of something missing while the years passed by and nothing changed. "You want to put money on that?"

Lara gave a low chuckle. "Okay, *you* probably could. But is that really what you want?"

It had been a long time since Cal had thought about what he wanted beyond a satisfying night and a job well done. Owen made him question everything.

"Just promise you'll give me a heads-up before making some big scene in front of Richard when you quit."

Now Cal had to chuckle. "Why, so you can keep the peace?"

"So I can *record* it."

He laughed outright. "I'm not going anywhere yet. And besides, Dick's an asshole... but he's a good man." Cal didn't need to make any scenes when he left, and was he seriously considering quitting? For Owen?

"Too bad all assholes aren't nice like us." She raised her glass for one more clink.

Cal obliged her, but his own swallow of beer was enjoyed slowly, because he wasn't entirely sure what he'd just admitted.

"Now, we playing darts or pool?" Lara rubbed her hands together as she glanced behind them, where both options waited. "Coz I'm having at least one more beer, and I owe you for that last poker match."

They had a mild rivalry with anything competitive, which came out in friendly games of cards or whatever else might be available. Lara was easy to be around in that sense, even when they weren't talking, something Cal had always appreciated about his friendship with Rhys too.

Which reminded him. "As long as you're being meddlesome, what's going on with Rhys? Dick said he's been clearing his schedule. You know anything about that?"

Lara smirked like she had a secret—and she *always* did. "Better ask him."


**OWEN** had to look on the bright side. Everything would be fine. Everything would be *fine*.

Plus, he had this insane text from Wesley—it still floored him that the mayor of Atlas City texted him on occasion—about a mob boss the police program had helped shut down, which was a huge win. He should have been overjoyed.

Harrison wasn't even in the building anymore, and still Owen jumped at shadows, expecting him around every corner. Maybe he was just being paranoid. He believed in predictability, because that's how models worked, and if analyzed correctly, they were almost never wrong. That didn't mean there weren't exceptions. The same was true of everyday life, like with Harrison showing up in his *office*. Sure, Owen had certain expectations based on past events, but Harrison could still prove to be an outlier and surprise him.

Maybe he really meant what he'd said, and at the end of it all, Owen would be able to put this behind him without any disasters.

"He slept with Marsh, ya know."

Jerking to a halt, Owen held back from continuing toward the vending machines as fear pumped through his veins. *What?*

"Seriously? He did?"

"Bet he's bangin' Walker too."

Those were two of the R&D guys, ones who'd been in the room with Owen and Harrison during the meeting. Were they talking about *him*?

"I don't think Adam's like that. He worships his wife."

"Fine, maybe Nye then. Hell, maybe the mayor!"

"Now you're reaching. Quinn's too sweet and reserved for that sort of thing."

They *were* talking about him.

"Please, the quiet ones are always freaks in private. You know that really good-looking guy he brings to all the events?"

"His publicist?"

"I heard he pays the guy for more than just managing his public persona, if you know what I mean."

*Oh God.* Was this what everyone had been whispering about?

"Really? Wow, guess you never know with some people."

Owen was going to throw up. A second ago, all he'd wanted was to devour the unhealthiest snack he could find to stifle his anxiety with calories, but now his stomach twisted like a sailor's knot.

The voices faded as the two developers walked on past the vending machines, but their words and implications remained. Owen didn't care what people thought about him, but rumors could still hurt his work, and if it got back to Cal or hurt *him* in any way, Owen would never forgive himself. Who had even started these rumors? Was it inevitable or made worse because Harrison was here?

They'd kept things quiet while they were together, at least at work, but some people had still whispered back in Middleton, and some knew. How else had Frank known when Owen started at Nye Industries? Owen hadn't cared about the whispers when he was with Harrison because he thought he was happy, kept trying to convince himself he was happy and that any scandal would be worth it.

Now he *was* happy, but the whispers were far more dangerous with much more at stake.

Owen needed to get ahead of this. He needed *help* to know how to handle shutting it down. But the first person he wanted to call, he couldn't, because all he felt like now was a burden.


**CAL** had taken out his contacts before leaving home, knowing how much Owen enjoyed the way he looked in glasses. He loved tying Owen's tongue with the right entrance. His outfit tonight was a tad dressy for the evening's plans, with slacks, a collared shirt and tie covered by a striped sweater he imagined fitting in well with Owen's new wardrobe—not that he wanted to distract himself with thoughts of Owen in *his* clothing—topped off with a smart gray blazer.

He wasn't *quitting* being an escort, certainly not tonight anyway, but if his schedule remained more open for a while and things between him and Owen shifted course, Cal wasn't going to hold back. Sometimes sticking to best-laid plans was overrated.

Expensive bottle of beer in hand, Cal knocked on Owen's door right on schedule.

An immediate answer didn't come.

Cal knocked again, thinking Owen might be in the bathroom or hadn't heard him, but a harried rush of footsteps soon followed, along with Owen's voice sounding agitated.

"I talked to Alyssa for over an hour, Mario." His voice carried through the door just before he wrenched it open. "I can't even think—*Cal*. What are you...?" Awareness hit him, and he looked guilty just like last night. "Dinner. You're scheduled tonight, and this time I really did forget. I'm *sorry*. Yes," he said into his phone, gesturing for Cal to come in as he continued fielding questions. "*No*, not right now, okay, can we just... I promise. I will. I love you too. Bye. I'm *sorry,* Cal," he said again, throwing his phone onto a crumpled pile of what Cal realized was Owen's jacket in the middle of the floor.

He looked—not terrible, but like the mess of the man Cal thought he was moving on from. Cal had been disappointed to find Owen well-adjusted last night because it worried him he was no longer needed, but seeing Owen like this again shredded him. His simple button-down and slacks were rumpled, shirt untucked, hair a mess like he'd been pulling at it for hours, eyes red, *face* red, just frazzled and fidgeting as he paced back toward him.

"I haven't even thought about dinner. I'm sorry, I didn't—"

"*Owen*." Cal shut the door behind him and looked at Owen squarely. "It's fine. Tell me what happened. I was ready to celebrate with you tonight after hearing about that crime boss the ACPD brought in, all because of your program." He lifted the beer to prove it.

"You were? You heard about that?" Owen lit up as if that almost made up for whatever was plaguing him. "It is good news, and it should be all I'm thinking about right now, but something else happened and I just... *urg*."

Taking the bottle from Cal and hurrying away again like he needed a moment to compose himself, Owen led Cal to the kitchen so he could put the bottle away, and Cal noted two normal-sized *empty* beer bottles on the counter.

Owen wasn't drunk, but the alcohol he'd tried to drown his sorrows in obviously hadn't helped soothe his nerves. After depositing the bottle in the fridge, instead of summoning a smile like Cal almost expected—not that he would have bought it—Owen plopped down on one of the island stools, elbows on the counter and head in his hands.

"Harrison's here. In Atlas City. At *Walker Tech*," he said before Cal could press him, and even though Cal's blood ran cold at the mention of that name, he maintained a calm temper while Owen explained the events of earlier that day, all the way to the rumors he'd overheard and how sorry he was if any of it got back to Cal's employer or got him into trouble.

Only Owen could have the devil at his back and snapping harpies all around him and worry about someone else.

"I called Alyssa, and Casey chimed in a couple times, then Mario called. All of them have different opinions about if I did the right thing agreeing to let Harry stay and work on the project. I don't know if I made the right choice, but what was I supposed to do? I keep thinking about how I'll have to see him again, who knows how soon or how many times, and I just…." His voice cracked, and he took a calming breath to slow down.

Cal had taken a stool next to Owen and used the pause in conversation to slide an arm around his shoulders. Owen accepted the embrace with a lean into his side. He'd been given enough advice for one night. What he needed now was a break.

"You hungry?" Cal asked.

"*Starving.*"

"Want to order a pizza?"

A helpless chuckle left him. "Not exactly the best pairing for that beer you brought."

"Beer is always good with pizza, Owen, that's Irresponsible Adolescence 101."

Another chuckle, followed by Owen peering at Cal fondly for making him laugh after so much drama. "Okay. You order, I'll open the beer."

"You sure you want another?" Cal nodded at the empty bottles.

Weary as he was, Owen looked at Cal with clear eyes. "As long as I can share it with you."

The bomber was only enough for a glass each anyway, but Cal still watched closely to be sure Owen didn't dip into intoxicated or grab another beer afterward. People thought they wanted oblivion in situations like this, but it was rarely the right call.

To his surprise, while Owen seemed to hit a nice buzz from the combination of what he'd drunk previously and Cal's offering, his eyes stayed focused, only his smile and posture proving he'd finally relaxed. The pizza arrived before they finished half their pours, and the last few sips paired perfectly with pepperoni, sausage, and sundried tomatoes.

They'd moved to the table when the food arrived, each in their customary chairs. Music played in the background now to cover any silences, and Cal's blazer hung over the chair behind him. He'd removed his tie as well, rolled up and shoved into his jacket pocket.

It was after Owen had downed his last swallow of beer and stared blankly at the empty glass, a little too far away and melancholic, that Cal asked a dangerous question.

"Do you still love him?"

Green eyes blinked at him in surprise. "*No*. I don't... think I do. I don't want to...." Then they clenched shut to stay the stubborn tears he'd been holding back. "Why do we *ever* love people we shouldn't?"

Cal had asked himself that question too many times. "It's not our choice who we love. Sometimes it's automatic. Love. Loyalty. But nobody's owed love, Owen, not even blood. Believe me, I know."

"You do?" Owen looked at him curiously.

Maybe *that* question was the dangerous one, because it prompted a response from Cal he'd never told any client. Yet with Owen, it seemed natural to undo the next few buttons on his shirt and tug it and his sweater down to show the faint line of his most prominent scar.

"Harrison broke your arm. I knew a man like him once. Broken collarbone, courtesy of dear old *Dad*."

The lingering haze of alcohol cleared from Owen's gaze. "Is he...?"

"Alive. In jail, actually."

"I'm sorry."

"It's where he belongs."

"What about your mother?" Owen asked, loose enough now to have less of a filter and not realize it.

Tonight should be about Owen. The evening was paid—it should always be about Owen. Not that Owen hadn't asked Cal personal questions before. Cal had told him plenty of stories about Claire, even Rhys, without going into anything about his friend's clients, but he'd always managed to avoid talking about his parents. Now, he didn't want to hold back, because Owen hadn't held back with him.

"I was about the age you were when your parents died... when my mother left. Claire was only a year then. She doesn't remember Mom at all. Says that made it easier, because she never had someone to miss. Maybe that's true, or maybe she's just good at making me feel better. Between Mom leaving and Dad being in and out of prison all my life, I kept it together focusing on my sister. Once Claire could take care of herself, I got as far away from my father as possible."

Cal wished *he* had another drink, even debated going to the fridge to get one, but that wasn't how this evening should end. Still, he couldn't help the way the expression on Owen's face made old resentments curdle in his stomach, because he didn't need anyone's pity.

"I know what you're thinking—ah, no wonder he sells himself with a messed-up background like that," Cal huffed, too honest when Owen deserved better than his baggage.

"I'd never think that," Owen said with a look that maybe wasn't pity, but Cal wasn't sure if he could trust what he read there. "I don't think it's wrong what you do. That's not why I don't want you to...." His cheeks flushed as he glanced away, obviously meaning Cal's more common escort duties. "But it's not something I'd ever shame you for. I know you stay safe. The agency makes sure of that. It's just a livelihood like anything else. As long as you enjoy what you do. As long as you're happy."

Just like Claire kept saying, because Cal insisted he *was* happy. Owen wasn't appeasing him, he meant those words, but Cal's response should have been automatic—*I am happy. I love what I do.*

Those words didn't come as easily anymore.

"I was never... good enough for my old man," Cal said, raw and open like *he* was the one on beer three. "Never made him happy. Never got any praise. Never *mattered*. Doing what I do now, I give people what they need, and no one ever looks at me like I haven't pleased them. I know that's messed-up." He looked toward Owen's view of the city. "But I like being that for someone."

"It's not messed-up. It's sweet," Owen said. "Maybe a little sad, but sweet. You make *me* happier." Flushing a darker scarlet, he glanced away as soon as Cal looked at him, sober enough to recognize his missing filter even if he was buzzed enough not to be able to control it. He seemed to come to terms with that, though, when his eyes flicked up. "You know, if I'm being honest with myself, I don't think I ever really loved Harrison. I just thought I did, because I didn't know what love was supposed to feel like yet."

Cal could definitely use another drink, but as he struggled with what to say in response, the playlist over the sound system beat him to it. "You Don't Know Me" started to play but it wasn't the Ray Charles version or any of the others Cal knew, though it was still sung in a smooth, male voice.

Owen leaned back and smiled as he listened. "You know what we've never done at all those fancy events?"

"Hm?"

"*Dance*. Will you dance with me, Cal?"

Cal laughed, but he couldn't say no to such an innocent request. "All right, Owen," he said, and stood to offer him a hand.

Giggling himself, Owen accepted it and let Cal pull him into the open space of the apartment. Cal slid his right hand around Owen's waist, but Owen shrugged him off and grabbed his right hand to stretch it outward.

"No, *I* lead," he said.

"And why is that?"

"I'm taller."

Cal snorted. "By a quarter inch maybe."

"Still counts," Owen said, holding firm to Cal's hand and sliding his arm around Cal's waist instead. "Larger person leads."

*Cal* was larger, even if only slightly, regardless of that quarter inch, but he conceded and rested his free hand on Owen's shoulder. "Okay, but just so you're prepared, I don't know how to do this backwards."

"I can do both, so I'll just have to teach you how to follow." The glow to Owen's cheeks brought on by the alcohol made it impossible to refuse him.

"Then lead on, Scarlet."

Owen led Cal into a simple foxtrot to follow the song, but even though Cal stepped forward several times and nearly crushed Owen's feet, he didn't falter, merely leaned into Cal so he stepped where he was meant to.

"How does a data scientist know how to dance so well?"

"I took ballroom in college," Owen said. "I loved it. Haven't gotten to show off my skills much lately, though."

They swayed and turned and moved across the floor, smoother with every verse. Cal had always loved and hated this song, because it was beautiful but sad. A tale of missed chances, of opportunities not taken. But Owen was right here, in his arms, their bodies touching in time with each step. Owen pulled him closer, near enough that their cheeks brushed.

Humming along with the song, he revealed a lovely voice to go with those dancing skills. There were still so many surprises he had in store for Cal.

He was stronger than he believed of himself. He'd still be slaying this new chapter in his life if not for Harrison showing up to toss it into chaos. Owen just needed to be reminded of that, of how precious and powerful he was, how worthy of the *love* Harrison had never truly given him.

Their hands drew inward, trapped between their chests, with Cal's other hand at Owen's neck, urging him closer until their foreheads pressed tight. Owen's humming faded, and the music drifted into the next song… just as Cal pushed past that last inch separating them and met his lips to Owen's.


**CAL** was *kissing him*. Owen almost tripped forward and toppled them both to the floor, but thankfully he froze long enough to turn any remaining attempts at dancing into swaying in place and then just… kissing.

"The Way You Look Tonight" overtook the previous song as Owen's lips parted, and he felt Cal's tongue press the advantage. It made him tremble to finally taste him, coffee and chocolate like the beer they'd shared and so *good*.

Owen's head was that perfect haze of cotton and clarity. His grip on Cal's waist tightened, just as Cal's grip on his neck did too. *This* was what he'd wanted. The way Cal tilted his head to push the kiss deeper, the low noise he made, the heat from his body, it was all so thrilling and perfect, just like last night when they hadn't tried to be anything but friends.

Unlike tonight—when Cal was being *paid*.

Owen's stomach twisted like being wrung out to dry. He was *paying* Cal for this. Cal was doing his *job* right now. A normal scheduled night because Owen was a client, not a friend. They weren't friends. He was such a fool.

"S-Stop," Owen gasped, pushing away from Cal until he stumbled backward. "I don't w-want you to d-do that. I didn't ask you to *do that*," he said more forcefully, not meaning to sound angry, but he was panting and flush and couldn't breathe after knowing Cal's embrace like that.

Shock and distress marred Cal's face, left standing with his hands hovering to mark the spot Owen escaped. "I'm sorry," he said, taking a step back as well. He looked mortified. "I've never gone against a client's wishes before. I should... I should go." Turning on his heels, he beelined for his blazer.

"Wait!" Owen chased after him but wasn't sure what to say. "*I'm* sorry."

Cal stopped, hand gripping the back of the chair with his jacket, and looked back at Owen over his shoulder. He always held himself together, poised and professional, but his face scrunched in this dreadful look of misery. "You don't need to apologize, Owen. This was my fault. It was careless of me. Habit."

Habit? Because Owen was a client and that's what Cal did for his clients. "R-right...."

How did that look of misery keep getting *worse*? "I didn't mean—"

"It's okay." Owen took a step forward because he had to fix this, even if it stung. He just wanted to fix this so Cal looked at him normally again, and they could pretend none of this ever happened. "You know, I don't want to think anymore tonight. Can we... can we curl up on the sofa and watch a movie?"

Cal sputtered a laugh, broken and false sounding. "Sure, Owen. We can do that." He turned to face him fully, but his hand hadn't left the back of the chair, and it was gripping so *hard*. "Whatever you want."

It stung worse when Cal started to take off his sweater, assuming Owen meant—

"*No*." He held out a hand for Cal to stop. "Just... like this. I want to stay dressed tonight. Okay?"

Everything Owen said, everything he tried to do to reset them seemed to make things worse. Cal's hands dropped to his sides, and his expression schooled into something managed and cold. It was *awful*. "Okay, Owen."

"S-stop that," Owen sniffled, unable to hold back the tears rushing to the surface. "I'm s-sorry, please don't l-look at me like that, I didn't *m-mean*—"

A blur swooped toward him, Cal moving so quickly as that stony mask dropped away to bring back the misery, but at least he soon had his arms wrapped around Owen to pull him closer. "Hey, shhh...."

Owen sobbed into Cal's shoulder harder than he had their first night together, holding him back so tightly, he feared he'd bruise him, but he couldn't help it. He always made things worse. He always made everything *worse*. But for weeks Cal had helped him believe that maybe he could get a few things right.

"It's okay. I'm sorry. We'll start over," Cal said with the softness and understanding Owen was used to. "Quiet night, just you and me, anything you want. I didn't mean to upset you. I was just angry at myself for making you uncomfortable. It's *okay*."

"R-really?" Owen nuzzled Cal's neck, wishing he wasn't leaving his shirt damp.

"*Really*. Come on." He smiled when he lifted Owen from his shoulder and brushed the tears from his eyes.

They sat on the sofa with Owen tucked against Cal's side. He pulled up the *Godzilla* movie, which should have been wonderfully silly, and they did laugh and point out moments they loved to each other, but it all felt tainted now, stifled in layers of things left unsaid.

Owen wished he could recapture what they had last night. He *wanted* to kiss Cal, but not when it was paid for, not when it was required. Despite the strides he'd thought they made before, he didn't know where they stood now.

It was the first time they ended a paid night without shedding any clothing, and instead of being optimistic when Cal left, Owen felt hollowed out and empty.

He'd ruined everything. Even if Cal wanted to kiss Owen outside of business, outside of money and obligation, he wouldn't want that after tonight. There was a cavern between them that Owen had deepened because he was too insecure to ask for what he wanted, even up to the moment when Cal left with that same press of lips to Owen's cheek but none of the same hope.

**CAL** knew now that he couldn't have his heart's desire, because when he'd tried to take it, that's when Owen, for all his understanding and attempts to care for Cal without judgment, for one unfair moment remembered what Cal was… and recoiled.

## *Chapter Eight*

**OWEN** had never seen someone punch the bag *off* the hook before—and he was the one who'd done it. He hadn't even been picturing Harrison's face, much as it would have been justified.

He'd been picturing his own.

"Everything all right?" Lorelei asked, retrieving the punching bag from the floor and hefting it up with impressive ease. He helped her lift it higher to rehang it on the hook.

"Not really," he said when he couldn't avoid looking at her, and went on to explain in as few words as possible how Harrison was in town and making his life miserable. He left out that his bad mood was more focused on someone else.

"Let's work on your disarming techniques," she said. "You've been getting better, but it's an important skill to master now that you've been using the shooting range. Most people won't mug you with only their fists."

"Okay...."

Waiting for her to retrieve a toy gun, which was sometimes replaced with a rubber knife, Owen followed her onto the mat. Each time she came at him brandishing the weapon, he dodged, deflected, or attempted to take the gun from her. He was fairly skilled now at succeeding when attacked from the front or side, but from behind it was still a challenge. He always tripped up in ways that would have caused the gun to go off or seriously cut him if his attacker had a knife.

"Wait... just... let me clear my head," he huffed after his third failed attempt to thwart her.

"Your head won't be clear in a real attack."

"I know, but—"

"*Instinct*. Confidence. Try again."

Two more times Owen failed. Then two times in a row... he succeeded. On the next attempt, he felt more assured, but as he readied himself for Lorelei's assault, it wasn't the gun he felt at his back but a hold on his left arm.

Alarm bells sounded in Owen's head, accompanied by something he didn't expect, because it wasn't fear that surged through him, it was anger.

Not recognizing the howl that left him until he spun, Owen whirled Lorelei around and pulled her tight to his chest. The gun dropped from her slackened grip, and he kicked her feet out from under her to slam her down to the ground. Glaring at her panting, *grinning* face, he realized with a rush what he'd just done.

"I'm sorry!" he reeled back before lurching forward again to help her up.

"Sorry?" She let out a boisterous laugh. "That's what I've been *waiting* for, Owen. You did it."

"I... did?" He blinked around them as if some other evidence needed to be discovered, but the proof had been there in the motion of his reflexes. "I *did*."

"And you're going to do it at least two more times before I let you go today."

*Urg*. Lorelei was the best, but she was also a little evil sometimes.

Instead of only two, Owen succeeded four out of five more times disarming her when she went for his weak spot, and the one time he missed, he'd still managed to knock the gun away. It made him excited to hit the shooting range next, a small but important win in what felt like a sea of losses.

"Cal's coming to the gala on Saturday, right?"

A sea Owen choked on when he remembered his biggest loss—though the water he'd been drinking going down the wrong pipe didn't help. "Uh... yeah."

Owen had scheduled Cal weeks ago for the event, so technically it was still planned, even though it would be the first time he'd see Cal again since last night. The next two days Cal was booked, and Owen felt the lack of him—and resented his time with other clients— more than ever before.

"I thought things were turning around for you two. Did something happen?" Lorelei asked. Her husband was on the state medical board, so they'd be at the gala as well. Owen loved the various ways his life intersected, like he was right where he should be, like it was *fate*, but the next few days felt rife with catastrophe because of how many pieces might collide.

Originally the gala was an excuse to have a Walker Tech and Nye Industries celebration publicly addressing the joint venture—combining efforts to usher in the next era in paralysis treatment and gene therapy for all sorts of ailments. This time Owen *would* need black tie. But that wasn't the problem. Given the involvement of Orion Labs going forward, Harrison would be there too. In the same room as Owen—and Cal.

Assuming Owen didn't cancel. Or Cal beat him to it.

"I think I ruined things," he said, always so easily honest with Lorelei because she had this way of looking through people without any judgment for what they might say.

"You *think* you did? You know what would probably help with that?"

"You don't even know what happened."

"Doesn't matter. It's usually the same answer. *Talk to him*." She pushed him playfully in the shoulder, causing him to chuckle miserably at the obvious but overwhelming suggestion. "He's a good guy. He's one of my sister's best friends, and she has very discerning taste. Plus, he obviously cares about you."

"I know." But what if they didn't care about each other the same way?

"If it's confidence you're lacking, I think it's time you took a long look in the mirror."

Leading Owen by the elbow, she directed him in front of a full-length mirror on the wall of the gym. He was sweaty, hair wilted, glasses smudged, but he couldn't deny how much more he filled out his damp Voltron T-shirt than he had a couple months ago.

"You're not the same man who walked away from Harrison Marsh and uprooted your whole life. You are *even stronger* than you were then."

She always said it like that—that he'd been strong all the way back on that night when he felt his weakest. Cal said it too, that Owen was braver than he knew. Maybe they were right and his biggest flaw was not believing it.

Squeezing his arm once more, she stepped out of view to leave him with his reflection. It wasn't just the added muscle he'd acquired from training that was different. He was independent now, successful, forming new relationships, and every last bit of it, he'd *earned*. He'd surpassed his fears in ways he never thought possible. He *had* changed, despite a few stumbles.

The last thing he wanted was to allow Harrison to ruin everything he'd built. But more than that, he didn't want *himself* to ruin it either.

Lorelei was right. He needed to talk to Cal.

**OWEN** had been messaging Cal all day but didn't want to talk over the phone. Cal had to reiterate that his schedule was booked until the party on Saturday, which wasn't a deflection. He had both Prince and Piper this week. There was very little time to see Owen, and he hated the idea of popping in to see him before either of those clients.

He wouldn't be able to get Owen out of his head if he did that.

He couldn't get him out of his head now.

Owen probably wanted to cancel Cal's services, but his good nature meant he wanted to explain in person. He didn't mean to judge—he hadn't *meant* to recoil from Cal's kiss—and Cal knew that, but Owen still didn't want to kiss someone who slept with people for money. If they couldn't get over that hurdle during one of the most intimate moments they'd ever shared, there was no getting over it in the future.

*I'll try to make time, Owen, but it might not be possible until Saturday.*

*That's okay! I understand. I just really want to talk to you. Don't forget black tie!*

At least Owen wasn't breaking their date for the gala, but Cal was certain it would be their last evening together. Maybe they could still be friends, but even if Owen wasn't planning to end things, Cal wasn't sure how much longer he could see Owen as an escort when he felt this way about him.

*Worse* was how that longing followed him to Prince's door.

Personal life was never meant to be carried to the "office," but Cal couldn't shake it, and Prince wasn't the type to miss even the slightest distraction.

The slow trail of her fingernails paused along their course up his thigh. "Calvin?" she prompted with a curious tone, "you are far away tonight. Our time together is hardly enjoyable with you so empty."

She was a vision in black lingerie, sheer lace up from her bra to a high collar around her neck, with a full garter belt and thigh-high stockings. Her long hair hung about her shoulders as she straddled him, tied with scarves to the bedposts but not yet blindfolded or gagged like she had planned.

Usually Cal was hard by now even with his underwear still on, anticipating the games she'd play that he had reveled in for far more months than he'd known Owen.

"You'll have to punish me, my dear," he said to banish his hesitation, "for daring to let my mind wander."

Prince had a lovely smile for all the fierce power in her eyes. "Usually I would agree with you, but I think I know where your mind has gone." She drew those same fingernails gently down the side of his face. "And I cannot compete. The beautiful boy with the innocent smile, yes?"

Cal felt a shred of alarm.

"People do take pictures at those events, you know," she said without any ill will.

Of course. He'd been in enough public spaces with Owen for his clients to have caught on, but he'd always prided himself on keeping each of them separate and special unto themselves. "When I'm with you, you are all I—"

"*Shush*. Don't disrespect me with lies no one would buy." Grabbing his chin, she held firm, dominant without ever being rough. "At first I found it curious, but your attention was still on me when I had you in my bed. Now it is with him, and I do not believe I can win you back."

While Cal struggled for how to respond, she released him and swung her legs off his hips to leave the bed.

"Selene…," he protested as she moved to untie the scarves.

"I can find another partner. My needs are more easily met than what you desire to fill the emptiness in your eyes. Go home. Your payment is still yours for tonight." She was the picture of ease considering the position they'd been in moments before, her hands swift but kind while undoing his bonds. "We do not control where our hearts wander. Perhaps you have a recommendation for a replacement?"

Cal knew Prince had a temper when it came to matters of personal justice or her people while working as an ambassador. He'd overheard a few severe phone conversations in various languages. But in situations like this, she was picturesque and admirable, which was part of why he'd accepted her as a client.

He sat up in bed after he was free, feeling strangely small and naked, considering his shorts had never left him.

"I… yes. Several," he said. He could think of at least three escorts who would suit Prince well, but he knew he'd disappointed her. She slipped on a red robe, tied loosely at her waist, and twisted her hair up into a swift bun, while her eyes traced his body with a hunger he'd always adored. "My apologies."

"You have nothing to apologize for. You always pleased me," she said, coming forward to sit beside him. "I would not want our last meeting to sully those nights together."

He'd let Owen into his head, let him disrupt his routine, his *work*, yet he was relieved Prince had called him on it. Still, it stung because: "I can't have him the way I want."

"No? Perhaps you are wrong, perhaps not. Either way, you aren't here tonight, so go." She reached for his face once more to feather fingers along his cheek. "Be alone with your desires until you decide which to pursue. If you darken my door again, I will welcome you. If not...." Leaning forward, she used the barest pressure to draw Cal toward her and kissed him soundly in goodbye. "I hope it means you found something worthwhile."

**"I CAN'T** believe you didn't tell me about this guy right away." Mario was worse than Alyssa sometimes when it came to petulance over being left out of the loop.

Or, Owen supposed, *lied to*.

"I didn't know what I wanted when I first started seeing him," Owen said. "There was nothing to tell."

"Seeing an escort on the regular is a *thing to tell* your best friend."

"I did tell you. Eventually."

Owen was at Walker Tech, ready to head home as he navigated the hallways and only talking hushed with Mario over the phone because his friend had been sending anxious text messages ever since their previous call was interrupted by Cal the other night. There were rumors going around the office that Owen had slept his way to his last position and was doing the same here—*and* at Nye Industries. He didn't need anyone overhearing his phone conversation about an escort when some people already whispered about Cal.

"Let me find a quiet corner." He cut Mario off from questioning him further. Normally, he'd tell his friend to call back later, but he needed another opinion. His mind had only been half on work for the past two days.

There were several quiet corners Owen knew about, both for recharge time when he needed to clear his mind and for fielding phone calls like this. He just needed to reach one, which happened to take him by the main conference room with clear glass walls looking directly inside.

Where *Harrison* was meeting with more of the development team.

"Harry's here." He skidded to a stop.

"Right now? Tell him I will kick his ass if—"

"He's in a meeting," Owen hissed into his phone. "Crap, it's ending. He saw me."

And he had the gall to smile all sweet and hopeful at Owen through the glass.

*Dick.*

*No*, Owen was the bigger man. He was giving Harrison the benefit of the doubt. He just didn't want to talk to him—ever. So, he nodded curtly and hurried on his way while returning to the conversation over the phone.

"Have you talked to him yet?" Mario asked.

"Not since he ambushed me at work the first time."

"No, I mean *Cal.*"

Owen sighed at the thought. Two days felt like forever with only emails between them. "Not yet. I need to see him in person, but he's been… booked."

"Sleeping with other people."

"It's what he *does*."

"And that doesn't bother you?"

"Not on principle." Owen clutched his phone tighter, trying to keep his voice soft with strained smiles given to the few people he passed. "Just the thought of anyone else touching him…."

"*Owen*," Mario admonished.

"I know, okay? This is a mess. But when you love someone, you have to let them live the life they want, not have them cater to what you'd make of them." It was one of Lorelei's many poignant lessons he'd taken to heart, because Harrison hadn't done that for him.

"Dude, I agree with you, you know I agree with you, but… did you just say you *love* him?"

Owen stopped like he had when he saw Harrison, then realized he'd come upon one of his favorite hidden nooks and ducked into it, a tiny hallway with a bathroom no one used and a stairwell for emergencies. He couldn't deny how easily that admission had left him.

"Shit. I *am* in love with him."

"*Shit*," Mario agreed.

Owen had the sudden feeling that someone was nearing his hiding spot, listening in or watching, but when he peered out into the hallway, he didn't see any shadows looming. He must be imagining things.

"If you really love this guy and being with him is what you want," Mario said, "I'll support you, man. I just don't want to see you hurt again. All those years with Harry…."

"I know. But Cal isn't Harry." Even if part of Owen had chosen Cal because of his age and poise and style being similar, everything else about him was solely Cal, and those were the things he loved about him. "If I love him, it has to mean I'll love him even if he only wants to be friends. Or if he does feel the same but wants to keep doing his job. I wish I could have him all to myself." He leaned back against the wall and imagined how wonderful that would be. "But as long as he could be mine because he wants to be with me, I think I could be okay with him being an escort forever."

CAL could not be an escort forever. Right now, he didn't want to be one at all.

He had to see Piper tonight. He and Owen hadn't even *talked* yet and he had no idea where they stood, but the last thing he wanted was for anyone other than Owen to touch him, especially after being let off the hook with Prince.

He'd forgone the usual errands he'd attend to during the day and secluded himself in his apartment ever since she sent him home. He knew what he wanted, but he doubted it would matter if Owen was planning to drop him after this weekend. If there was some dramatic gesture he could carry out to change that, he'd try anything, but he couldn't rely on his usual seductions. Everything was so much harder when *feelings* were involved.

A knock at the door surprised Cal. He'd wasted the day away debating what to do. Soon he'd have to get ready to see Piper, since calling in sick was not an option.

Heading for the door, he assumed it was mail put in someone else's box or some other bland interruption, but he realized his mistake when he yanked the door open to find Rhys on the other side.

"I pulled the plug."

"What?" Cal gawked, having no idea what he was talking about.

"*Frost*." Rhys pushed past him into the apartment, more animated than usual, which was saying something for *Rhys*. "I told her I loved her, then went straight to Nick of Time to give up my last client and told Dick to *shove it* if he has a problem."

Cal pivoted slowly after shutting the door, gawk far more prominent. "You're *quitting*?"

"Course not," Rhys snorted. "I love this gig. Just stickin' to actual escort clients from now on. Dani wouldn't ask me to change, but I wanna be all hers—only hers. Told her that, told her what I wanted, and *damn* can that girl kiss."

Cal couldn't keep the smile from his face when he saw the way Rhys lit up talking about her. "Dani?" He called him on the casual drop of his client's name.

Rhys sobered, then shrugged like he'd come this far so there was no reason to hold back. "Danielle. Doll's a *doctor*."

Cal chuckled. He and Rhys didn't *share*, they exchanged crib notes more than the deep recesses of their hearts, but it was oddly freeing. "Owen," he said to keep them even. "The one busy saving Atlas City."

"*Quinn?*" Rhys sputtered after turning that over. "Damn, he's Scarlet, huh?"

"Apparently, we're in at least one society article together."

"Like I read that shit. Good on you, though. Wait, so *yer* quittin'?"

"No," Cal answered reflexively, finally moving from the door. Then he had to wonder. "I don't know. I don't think he wants me. I want him, but he... he backed away like my lips gave him freezer burn."

No, they didn't share. It wasn't the sort of friends they were, at least not without a few shots between them, but still Rhys asked, "What happened?"

So Cal told him—everything about the night he finally stole a kiss. "He means well, but he can't see past what I am."

"That is the stupidest thing I ever heard," Rhys said.

"He didn't want to kiss me," Cal growled. "I pushed, with a client, against the arrangement we'd made, and he backed off like he couldn't get away fast enough."

"Yeah, coz it was a *paid* night, idiot."

"That's what I'm *saying*. He doesn't want to be with someone who sells themselves, no matter how much he wishes it didn't bother him."

"Or"—Rhys leaned menacingly into his space— "he didn't want to kiss you on a night he paid you coz he was afraid that was the only reason you did it."

The air rushed from Cal's lungs even as he opened his mouth to counter, until nothing could be said other than, "I'm an idiot."

"Yer an idiot."

"I'm seeing Piper tonight." He stared at Rhys wide-eyed. "I *can't* see Piper tonight."

"Listen, pal"—Rhys picked up on the rational side since, for once, Cal was the one flailing—"Dick's gonna be pissed. Maybe Piper too. But yer head's already outta the game. You got it bad. Time ya did somethin' about it."

"Easy for you to say. Your gamble paid off."

"Well I am prettier than you." Rhys smirked, encompassing everything Cal loved about his friend. "But I'm sure the universe'll give ya a break."

Pretty was not one of Rhys's traits, but he was almost never wrong, and if he could admit when he'd fallen for a client, who was Cal to pretend otherwise or deny the evidence that Owen might want him in return? It didn't mean the universe had his back, but it did mean that thoughts of Owen didn't merely follow him to Piper's door; they led the way.

He'd been practicing since the moment he left home how to explain to the young musician that they would *not* be going through their normal routine tonight. Cal even had a few replacements at the ready. He had the power to drop any client he wished, but he owed Piper more than that after so long together, never a disappointment, never a problem. He didn't want things to end sourly between them.

Mouth poised to talk instead of kiss as soon as the door opened, Cal's words were stolen by the sight of Piper. Normally, he answered his door in simple clothing, maybe even a robe, since he'd be showering for the concert after their encounter, but tonight Piper was smartly dressed and already smelling of aftershave.

"Heading to the concert early?" Cal asked, though Piper wasn't wearing his tux. He didn't look surprised like he'd forgotten Cal was coming either.

"I don't have a concert tonight," he said.

"You don't?" If Piper had his heart set on *experimenting*, he was going to be much harder to let down gently.

"Come here, handsome. Let's chat."

Cal should head this off now and explain before Piper went into detail about the carnal activities he had planned. He wasn't prepared for what Piper actually said once they sat on the sofa.

"I want a job."

"Excuse me?" Cal tried to process that statement. "Doing what?"

"With *you*. I want a job at the agency."

"You…." For a moment, Cal was floored. Then all the ways Piper tried to immerse himself in anything his parents deemed *unseemly* came to the forefront, and he stared back unimpressed. "We don't take bratty kids who just want to piss off Mommy and Daddy."

"Please. That's just a bonus. I'm done with the philharmonic. I want more freedom with my schedule and entertainment for my evenings—with a paycheck. Of course it means we wouldn't see each other anymore, which would be a huge loss." He trailed his fingers down Cal's arm. "Though… maybe…?"

"I don't sleep with coworkers." Cal put that notion to bed, much as he appreciated the young man's pluck. "A working relationship would be the end for us. Though I suppose I could help you get started, find the right clientele for an initial spread, put in a good word with the CEO…."

It was crazy—a client asking for a referral to *become* an escort—but if anyone could do it, Piper was a prime candidate. Not only was he attractive, he was also well-educated, well-dressed, and very well-versed in the bedroom.

"You're serious?" Cal pressed. "Because I wouldn't offer a recommendation if I didn't think you'd make an excellent addition to the catalog, but I also need to know this isn't some game."

"I'm serious." Piper nodded eagerly.

Maybe the universe *was* on Cal's side. He wished he could rush right over to Owen's apartment, free and clear of all his clients, but their reunion would have to wait. Tonight Cal had to make his exit plan, and being able to offer Piper as a replacement would ease Dick's reaction significantly.

"Your evening's free?" Cal asked.

"All yours," Piper said.

"Then listen up, coz I am taking you in tomorrow morning, and you need to be ready to impress the boss."


**PART** of Owen had hoped Cal would be able to see him before the gala. Another part was glad he'd had more time to think about what to say, especially since he'd purposely gotten a new tux without Cal's help—though he had used Dennis—so he could surprise him. He wanted to make *Cal's* jaw drop for once.

It was just a normal tux, simple black with a white shirt, but it fit him flawlessly, very James Bond. Owen had debated wearing his gold glasses again but decided the black ones made more sense with black tie. He'd gotten a haircut, brunet poof coifed to perfection, wore new cologne, had on his nicest watch. He looked *good*. Even he could admit that.

A timely knock at the door finally came, and Owen took a breath before opening it that immediately caught in his throat.

Cal was stunning. He also wore a black tux, but his shirt was deep navy. The glasses were back for his "White" persona as Owen's publicist, and the gray wool coat Owen remembered from their first meeting pulled it all together.

Yet, as gorgeous as he looked, Owen had succeeded, because Cal stood gaping too.

"Well *done*, Owen. You'll turn every head at the party."

"Y-you too."

Common sense fled Owen when he was this nervous, so the déjà vu continued as he forgot to invite Cal in right away but kept staring. With a chuckle as he caught himself and gestured Cal inside, the awkward pause that stretched between them was near unbearable until both he and Cal started speaking at the same time.

"Look, I'm sorry for how I—"

"Owen, I need you to understand—"

They cut off, laughed at how ridiculous they were being, and tried again.

"You first," Cal said.

All of Owen's practicing amounted to a single phrase. "I'm sorry I made things weird."

"I'm sorry *I* did."

"It wasn't because of your job."

"I know. I'm sorry that, for a moment, I thought otherwise." Taking Owen's hand with slow, telegraphed movements, Cal lifted it to his lips and kissed the back of his fingers, causing Owen to blush deeply scarlet. "Why don't we pretend that evening between friends happened only last night and *tonight*... is also unpaid."

"What? You don't have to—"

"I *want* to enjoy tonight as friends. So we know that anything that happens is only what we both want." Dropping Owen's hand between them, Cal held on to his fingertips. "Then later, after the gala, when we have more time, there are some things I want to discuss with you. Okay?"

"Good things?" Owen asked, as goose bumps prickled along his arms beneath the tux.

"I hope so," Cal said.

Owen's heart was beating so fast he almost surged forward to kiss Cal right then. But no. Not yet. *After* they talked, which he was suddenly very much looking forward to. "O-okay."

Like a true gentleman, when Cal at last released Owen's fingers, he offered his arm instead. "Shall we?"

Owen grabbed his jacket from the rack by the door and accepted Cal's arm, feeling the heavy weight on his shoulders finally lift.

This part they had down—attending an event together, wowing the crowd, mostly with Cal doing the wowing and Owen playing catch-up, but they balanced each other well. Cal had even prepared several notes for Owen in case he was asked to say a few words during the announcement. He never would have been able to write his own speeches.

The gala was in a real ballroom, dazzling with colored lights, men in their tuxes, women in gowns. There was even dancing, another nod from the universe that Owen thought unfair and all too tempting.

Since the event was buzzing with Nye and Walker employees, every time someone's eyes landed on Owen, he wondered if their whispers were those same rumors circulating. He'd been thinking hard about that problem too.

"As your publicist, I advise you to get ahead of these rumors... by admitting to them," Cal whispered after another group of people kept staring.

"I was thinking the same thing," Owen said. "Not about *you*. I'd never—"

"Preferably, you'll avoid breaking the contract you signed with Nick of Time, but if you ever needed to...," he trailed, giving Owen an out he never intended to use.

"That's not what I meant. I think—"

"Owen!" Keri's voice cut through the crowd, and seeing as how she—and Adam trailing beside her—were the guests of honor, everyone parted to let them through. Somehow, even though the two CEOs weren't touching each other, there was an air of Keri having dragged Adam by the ear.

"Everything okay?" Owen asked.

"*Adam* would like to apologize," Keri said.

"Umm…." Owen blinked in confusion. "…okay. What did—"

"I never would have agreed to meet with Marsh if I knew you used to *date* him," Adam blurted.

*Oh God.* The rumors had reached Adam? Or was it just that Keri had always known? The look on her face said she had, whether from long before or because Frank was, well, *Frank*.

"I know this looks bad," Owen said, keeping the small circle of him, Cal, Adam, and Keri close-quartered, "that I slept with an executive even if he wasn't my boss, but I swear we started dating *before* I worked at Orion Labs. Which… actually looks *worse*…." He realized with a grimace.

"Owen," Keri said, "I'm married to the mayor. You think they haven't tried crucifying us for nepotism on occasion. People will always talk. I couldn't care *less*—"

"Same here!" Adam said emphatically. "We know you earned your place. Your work proves that and so does your integrity. Exes can be a messy business, especially office romances. Was it messy?" He dropped his voice lower. "Is he trying to make trouble for you?"

"Because if he's threatened you in any way—" Keri jumped in.

"*No*. He hasn't." The pair of them were very sweet, but Owen had to end this. "It *was* messy, but he hasn't done anything to warrant ignoring the proposal. We should move forward with Orion Labs."

"Are you sure?" Keri questioned.

"This is a huge endeavor. I can't let my love life get in the way of that."

The two CEOs seemed assuaged, but Keri still crossed her arms with prominent authority. "Just remember my husband is the mayor if you need someone killed."

Owen chuckled. "I don't want Harry *dead*." Much as he might have fantasized about some horrible accident befalling him.

"I meant *Adam*." She glared at her counterpart.

Hunched in on himself from his usually towering height, Adam looked like a scolded child. "There are several social cues I've been told I need to work on. I'm really sorry, Owen."

So many people were looking out for him. Owen had always had people looking out for him, and he appreciated that more than he'd ever be able to tell them, but now it was time to look out for himself.

"Thank you. All of you. But actually, I was about to get Cal's opinion on something. I have an interview at your offices on Monday," he said to Keri. "I think I should tell the truth about dating Harrison. *Publicly*. I've been giving it a lot of thought, and it's the only way to avoid more rumors—by owning them."

Owen didn't expect Cal to argue the point, but Adam and Keri surprised him by not countering either.

"Whatever you want, Owen."

"We'll support you."

It reminded him why he'd wanted to work with their companies in the first place.

When the pair finally headed back into the crowd to continue playing hosts, Cal asked him, "Are you also going to admit what he did to you?"

"No," Owen said. "Maybe he *is* a snake, but if he means all this about making it up to me, I don't want to ruin him. Admitting we dated looks bad enough, but most people won't care after a week. I have another chance here in Atlas City. Part of me hopes he can find that too."

The look Cal gave Owen was both amazed and adoring, causing a fresh blush to creep up his neck. "And another part of you wouldn't mind setting him on fire?"

Owen laughed. "Do you think any of the mob bosses my program hasn't caught yet do the whole cement-shoe thing?"

Cal snickered with him. It was nice to make light of something that had so recently haunted him. He didn't want any ghosts from his past hovering over his future. He just wanted to move on.

Naturally, it was right then, while noticing Lorelei and Tommy across the room with Frank and Paul, that Owen also spotted Harrison headed toward them. He clutched Cal's arm so tightly, the other man knew instantly what had spooked him.

"That's him?"

"Yeah."

Harrison's tux was simple too, classic and flattering at every angle. Still several yards away, his eyes were focused right on them.

"I don't think he's too happy about me," Cal said.

"Really? Maybe it's not so bad. He's smiling."

"A dangerous smile. I know how to read people. If you want to steer clear—"

"No." Owen held his ground, waiting for Harrison to come to them. "I won't run scared anymore. That's the whole *point*. He says he wants to make things up to me, so I want to let him. If he's an asshole, *then* we can set him on fire."

Cal snorted but didn't dissent, allowing this decision to be Owen's.

It felt like one of those moments in a disaster movie, when the meteor headed toward Earth was just about to make impact.

"Owen," Harrison said as he reached them, eyes dragging openly down Owen's body, though not crudely so. "You wear a tux well. Never thought I'd see you in one. You hate ties."

Four years together meant Harrison *knew* him, but that didn't change anything that had happened. "A good tailor makes a big difference."

"Is that who's on your arm?" Harrison's attention strayed to Cal with a tighter pull on his jaw. "Your *tailor*?"

Cal smiled cordially while offering his hand. "Cal White. Owen's publicist."

"Of course. I've heard so much about you." The meteor collided with the touch of their skin, but no explosions erupted. Owen wondered if either of them fell prey to that old trick of trying to crush the other person's hand, and if they did, he hoped Cal won.

Wait, Harrison had *heard* about Cal? He'd just gotten here. "From who?"

"People talk." Harrison shrugged before shifting his gaze to Cal once more. "Quite a bit actually. He must pay you well to attend all his events like this."

"Owen is an ideal client but also a friend. And I hate to leave my friends alone in distasteful situations."

Oh, Owen *loved* Cal. He really did.

"Good thing it's such a lovely party," Harrison said, then snapped his gaze to Owen. "Would it be too *distasteful* to speak with you in private? It's important or I wouldn't ask."

That old shred of panic returned, but Owen knew the only reason Harrison continued to have power over him was because he allowed it.

"We're still making the rounds, actually, so I'm afraid—" Cal stepped in to Owen's rescue, but he couldn't keep letting people do that.

"Cal. It's okay." Meeting Cal's concerned expression, he pulled in close to whisper, "Five minutes, so he stops hounding me. Better here than some corner at the office. But if he tries anything…. *Fire*."

That garnered the appropriate response, because Cal smiled back but still said quite seriously, "*Five* minutes," before letting him go.

Owen put his foot down when Harrison tried leading him out of the ballroom. He was not stepping into any dark hallways with him, *ever*, but he compromised by ducking into an alcove that gave them the privacy Harrison wanted while still allowing Owen an easy getaway back into the throng.

"What do you want?" Owen asked.

Without pause or an attempt at small talk, Harrison dropped his serene expression for a look of desperation. "You can't trust that man."

*Unbelievable.* "I came with you because I thought you were serious about being better, about not trying to manipulate me, and you immediately—"

"It's dangerous," Harrison insisted. "You can't trust him. Do you even know what he is?"

*"What* he is? You—"

"Because I do. Check your email."

That caught Owen up short, because what game did Harrison think he was playing? Owen had planned to warn him that he was going to admit the truth about their relationship, and right away, Harrison was back to old tricks.

Still, out of morbid curiosity, Owen pulled his phone from his pocket to take a look. Unsurprisingly, he had a new email from Harrison. But it wasn't a message. It was a video.

"What is this?" There was no revealing thumbnail, so all Owen saw was a black screen and a Play button.

"Watch it. Then you'll see."

Maybe there were more meteors headed Owen's way. He didn't want to give in to Harrison, but he pressed Play anyway if only to prove whatever the man hoped to achieve here wrong.

The black screen brightened to show a bed from a wide angle. Then, moments later.... *Cal* dropped down on top of it. He was half dressed and being swiftly removed of remaining clothing by another man climbing after him.

For one horrible, heart-stopping moment, Owen thought the man was *Harry*, but even though Owen could only see the man from behind, he knew he was too broad to be Harrison, just strangely familiar.

The audio came through as breathless panting and plaintive whines like no noises Owen had ever heard from Cal. Then the other man started giving... *commands*, and Cal obeyed every one without question.

*Hands above your head.*

*Arch your neck.*

*Yes....*

*Like that.*

*Such a beauty you are, Calvin.*

*So well behaved.*

Owen wanted to throw his phone down, because he shouldn't be watching this—why did it even exist, and why was that man so familiar, especially his profile when he turned toward the camera that Cal obviously didn't know about—but Owen couldn't stop staring at the footage.

**CAL** tried to keep an eye on Owen when he disappeared into the crowd, but he lost him to the throng and constant movement of black tuxes and flowing dresses. He debated his options. If he followed, he'd be ignoring Owen's wishes. The last thing he wanted was to alienate Owen now.

After all, he'd *quit* that morning.

Checking his watch, Cal decided to do exactly as they'd agreed. Give him five minutes, *then* go looking. Maybe in the meantime he could find Lorelei or—

"Hello, Calvin."

*Merlin.*

Slowly turning to stare at the man who'd snuck up on him while his mind was on Owen, Cal discovered his former client looking dapper and snide as always. "Sterling. What a *displeasure* to see you again. Still sore about your cold bed?"

"Not for long," he said cryptically. "I just wanted to say hello. Though I'm fairly certain soon it will be... goodbye." Tilting his head in the direction Owen had gone, he added, "That boy of yours is exquisite. Pity he ran off."

The threat was easy to interpret, but Merlin didn't head Owen's direction—he moved for the exit. Clearly, like he'd said weeks ago, *he* wasn't the one Owen had to watch out for.

Cal needed to find him. *Now.*

**"WHY** do you have this?" Owen asked, nauseated even as he continued watching the video on his phone. He felt lewd seeing Cal stripped bare and on display, unaware of the camera as he played a more submissive role to suit this client—moaning, *begging*.

"Do you see what he is now?" Harrison's voice filtered into the tiny bubble Owen was trapped in. "I didn't want to show you this, but I needed you to understand the truth once I realized how much trust you'd put in someone who is only playing a role."

Owen barely heard him, too focused on the video, because he knew that other man from somewhere….

"*Owen*," Harrison prompted louder, as a hand took hold of his chin to tilt it upward. Harrison was too close, and Owen had a wall at his back from keeping the phone pointed away from the ballroom. "I wish I could stay away, that I could give you the space you've asked for, but you are everything to me. Don't you understand that? I haven't let anyone else touch me all these months waiting for you to come home."

Trying to back out of his hold, Owen only ended up deeper into the alcove *away* from the crowd, and Harrison pursued him. The sound of the video, the thoughts plaguing Owen that he knew the other man's face, disrupted his focus when his instincts should have been to push Harrison away.

"I miss you." He crowded in closer. "Don't you miss me? Don't you miss being with someone worthy of you?" And he descended to steal a *kiss*.

Owen froze and hated himself for freezing because he'd come so *far*. He was starved for the feeling of another's lips on his, and for a brief flash of memory, he recalled why these lips were ones he'd longed for.

But now the only ones he wanted were Cal's.

He didn't care about the roles Cal played in the past, because he knew the man he was with tonight was the real Cal, even wearing glasses and sporting a fake name. Cal wasn't defined by his job. No one was, no matter what their livelihood. Having seen that footage didn't change anything in Owen's mind about his friend other than stir up jealousy because *he* wanted to be the one causing Cal to make noises like that.

The hand with the phone dropped to Owen's side, but the other came up to grip Harrison's tux, ready to shove him away... just as he remembered why that other face looked familiar.

It was Cal's former client. In footage that shouldn't exist. And Harrison had the footage.

The *snake*. The no-good, rotten—

"Always knew there was something off about Merlin." Cal's voice interrupted before Owen could heave Harrison off him. He pushed him away now and turned toward the ballroom where Cal stood—staring at the phone in Owen's hand that was turned outward to reveal the blatant footage of—

"*No*." Owen pulled the screen to him to hide the telling image. But it wasn't telling! Owen wasn't in cahoots with Harrison, watching that footage out of some sick gratification. "Cal—"

"Who'd guess it was a camera in the bedroom? Which is *against* the contract he signed, by the way." Cal smiled, empty and awful like the other night— *worse*. "Same as the one you signed. But then you only hired me for Merlin's payback, didn't you? Have a good rest of your evening, Owen," he said, and with a cold nod, he turned on his heels and fled.

"Cal, wait! Please!" Owen lurched to move around Harrison, but the other man gripped his shoulders to hold him in place.

"Let him go. Listen to me."

"This is your fault!" Owen knocked him back, only for Harrison to raise his hands in surrender, as if, once again, Owen was the one being unreasonable.

"This is not how I planned for things to go, but all the better if it rids you of that man."

*Planned?*

Owen stared at the video, paused now but easily displaying the face of Cal's client, Merlin, as the truth rushed through calculations in his brain and the patterns fell into place—so obvious now, all the way back to the beginning.

"You *know* him. You used Cal's client to start those rumors to make me think I needed you. You started them weeks ago when I wouldn't email you back. It just took this long for them to pick up steam. And you only started emailing me because you saw I was moving on without you."

Shaking his head, Harrison wore such an earnest lie of an expression, but his words didn't deny what Owen had said. "None of this was to hurt you. I was trying to *protect* you."

"*Screw you*, Harry," Owen snarled as he shoved his phone into his pocket.

A twitch of malicious truth flickered across Harrison's face. "You're the one *screwing* a prostitute. Do you know how that could ruin your career? Ruin everything you think you've built here? Yes, I know Sterling. He has friends in many places, including at Walker Tech and Nye Industries. When we realized our interests connected, we saw an opportunity—"

"Because you're a snake!" Owen shouted, unable to think of Harrison as anything else. "Because using people is all you know how to do. But I'm not yours anymore, Harry, and I am never going to be yours again."

Pivoting to move out of the alcove—Owen had time, he could still catch Cal—he was ready to leave Harrison and any thoughts of "benefit of the doubt" behind.

"You don't know what you're saying. You *do* need me," Harrison said, and before Owen could clear the corner, firm fingers wrapped around his left arm.

Instinct took over in place of panic, and with a twist and inward pull to whirl Harrison around, Owen rushed back into the alcove and slammed him face-first into the wall. His heart beat wildly, but he wasn't afraid. *He wasn't afraid.*

"No, Harry. I don't."

Pushing forward once more to leave Harrison against the wall, Owen used the momentum to spring out of the alcove and move at a near-run along the edge of the ballroom. He couldn't let things end like this. He *wouldn't.*

There was no sign of Cal at the door or by the coat check, but if he *had* stopped to retrieve his coat, he couldn't have gotten much of a head start. Leaving his own jacket behind, Owen escaped into the night to find Cal no matter how long it took.

## *Chapter Nine*

**THEY'D** taken a cab to the gala. Cal should find one now, get home, put this behind him, and figure out how to salvage what he'd ruined of his life. Dick had sighed at him in exasperation that morning when he came in with a *client*, saying he was leaving.

"Not *for* my client," he'd explained with a gesture at the young man beside him. "I have my reasons, but before you jump down my throat for quitting, consider my replacement."

Given Cal's departure had been less heated than Rhys's—and Rhys hadn't *left*, just changed his type of clientele—Dick was reasonable about making an exchange for a new escort instead of losing one.

Maybe he'd be willing to take Cal back since it hadn't even been twenty-four hours. Cal should call the office now, get ahead of this, whatever he needed to do as he escaped the building behind him and how Owen had been conning him from day one.

Cal blacklisted an unsavory client and in less than a week got a request from a new one who monopolized his time and never wanted more than a snuggle? How had he been so *stupid*? He'd given up everything for Owen, and it was all just some game between him and Harrison—and *Merlin,* with his camera and who knows how many videos they'd watched to get their kicks.

Scrounging for his cell phone, Cal thought to dial Lara or maybe even Dick directly just as two teardrops landed on his coat sleeve. *No.* Owen did not deserve this reaction, to have broken Cal so thoroughly, just because he'd been sweet and Cal had... *thought....*

"Cal, wait!"

*I'm sure the universe'll give ya a break.*

"Cal!"

Yeah right. The universe was a *bitch*, and fate meant being the joke everyone else laughed at.

Scrubbing furiously at his face to hide the evidence, Cal kept walking, no destination in mind, just *away* from that voice and every lie that came with it.

"Cal, please! Stop! It's not what you think!"

Even caught in the act, he thought he could swindle Cal again? Not a chance.

"*Please*," Owen huffed as he caught up to him, not trying to touch—*smart move*—but staying close. He didn't have his coat, just the tux, with the cool air making his breath come out as billowing puffs.

Cal ignored him, paused only a moment at a crosswalk on red, then continued forward once the light changed. He didn't even know what street he was on anymore. The traffic, other people moving the opposite direction, *Owen*—it was all a blur.

"Talk to me." Owen stayed in step with him. "Just talk to me, Cal. Let me explain."

"This was all for Merlin." Cal held his voice steady, staring straight ahead. "You are *good*, Owen. Booked me the same week I dropped him. I should have known."

*"No.* I don't know Merlin. I didn't even know Harry knew him. You have to believe me!"

Another crosswalk, already on green, which Cal blew through and then took a sharp right to drive the point home that he wanted nothing to do with Owen's schemes.

But Owen was persistent.

"I hadn't seen that video until tonight, or any videos. Harry was trying to turn me against you, but seeing something like that could never turn me against you, Cal. He had me cornered. I didn't want to kiss him. It was just... bad timing!"

"Bad—" Cal came up short at the sheer gall of Owen's excuses, but when he whirled to face him, he faltered at the look of sincerity on Owen's face, already chapped red from the wind.

A *lie*. It had to be a lie. A convincing *act*.

"I know what I am," Cal said. "What I've been. People think they can use me, and why not? In their minds, I let others use me every day. Being used is how I make a living. But at least it's on my terms. To think, the first person who ever made me feel like a *whore*, I've never even slept with."

Owen reared back, so convincingly hurt that Cal waited for the waterworks, for the con to ramp up again, yet it was somehow worse that Owen's eyes clouded, dampened, but he didn't cry. "You don't really believe I could think of you that way, do you?"

*Damn.* He was good. Too good. Too... believable.

Cal tried to back up, but there was an alley behind him, and he wasn't sure which direction to go. Approaching footsteps made Owen's head jerk to the left, where a shadowed man headed their direction. There were hardly any people around now, the streets very different from only a few blocks down where high society was enjoying a night out.

Snapping his attention back to Cal, Owen still didn't shed any tears but looked resolute as he surged forward to grip Cal's arms and pushed him into the alley. Cal would have fought back, pushed Owen in return, or at least wrenched his arms away, but he found his reflexes stolen by Owen's touch.

"You don't believe that." His eyes carried potent emotion. "I know you don't. You're hurt, and all the evidence fell together the wrong way. But this is what I'm good at—building a picture out of the data, the *real* data, and you need the whole story to do that. Just like my models, telling me certain streets are more likely to see muggings. Like... this one, actually." He scanned the narrow alley he'd pushed them down with a shred of trepidation. "Uhh... maybe we should—"

Cal heard the click before he noticed the shadow behind Owen, but it was the way his eyes widened that told him a *gun* had just been pressed to Owen's back.


**THIS** wasn't happening. Owen had spent months, *years* working out the data models to predict things like this, and he'd still walked into crime alley—literally.

He could feel the weight of the gun in the press of its barrel against his spine.

"Ain't you two dressed up nice?" the voice behind him said, playing at being friendly. "Get turned around leavin' the party, hoss? That's too bad. I'd be happy to give ya directions, but you're gonna have to give me somethin' first. Your *wallet*." He jabbed Owen harder with a shift in tone. "Yours too, Wall Street."

Cal raised his hands slowly, eyes glowing brighter in the dark as his indecision, anger, and grief washed away in place of fear while he moved to obey.

"Hurry up." The gun jabbed Owen again.

"I-I don't have my wallet." His hands trembled as he raised them in kind. "I left it in my other jacket."

"You wanna play that game?" the voice asked more dangerously just as Cal held his wallet out.

"I swear!" Owen raised his hands higher. "Please. You don't want to do this anyway. Trust me."

"Oh yeah?" Warm breath struck Owen's ear with a humored puff. "Coz you're some big shot, that it?"

Cal's eyes screamed at Owen to give the mugger something, anything—the *watch*, he nodded at his wrist with insistence.

*I know what we've been training for, Owen, but unless you can be 100 percent certain about a disarm*, Lorelei's voice broke into his thoughts, *don't try it. Just give your attacker what they want.*

He should, wallet or no, but he hesitated to offer anything when he was poised to lose so much more.

"Because this alley is within a five-block radius of high recorded criminal activity," Owen said as his trembling came under control. "With a publicized event occurring three blocks South, the ratio of police patrols is tripled from other locations around the city. If you fire that gun, there's at least one squad car close enough *right now* to hear it. They'll catch you in minutes."

Laughter sounded from behind him. "You tryin' to scare me with that techy talk? Not gonna happen. Play nice like your buddy here."

"I can't do that."

"*Owen*," Cal pleaded.

"Listen to your friend, hoss. You don't wanna be a hero tonight."

Cal's eyes implored him with equal weight, but Owen couldn't be sure if that meant he believed him or was just a good man.

"Sometimes running is the brave thing," Cal said, calling on a private moment that made Owen smile with a shred of hope.

"I know."

"Good boy," the mugger said, assuming Owen was ready to listen. But as he reached over Owen's shoulder to take Cal's wallet, "Now—" Owen sprang into action.

Left hand coming up to catch the mugger's wrist, his right reached back in sync to grab the gun arm, twisting his body in the same motion to point the gun at the ground in case it went off. It didn't.

Pivoting the rest of the way around, Owen jammed his shoulder into the mugger's chest, staggering him back, and peeled the gun from his fingers. The man had the mouth of the alley behind him as well as the street, while Owen held the gun and pointed it square at his chest. He gestured for the mugger to move against the wall, and just like that, Owen had control.

He owed Lorelei a drink.

"Sometimes running *is* the brave thing," he repeated, "but tonight was not the night to push me."

"Whoa, man." The mugger's hands shot up. He had on dark clothes, a sweatshirt with the hood up, but no bloodshot eyes like some junkie. "Hang on—"

"I don't want to run anymore," Owen spoke over him, but even as he kept the gun on the attacker, he shifted his focus to Cal. "And I'm not letting you run, either. I mean… if you still want to go after you hear what I have to say, I won't stop you, but please, let me explain."

Cal's expression was as startled as the mugger's. His arms dropped, wallet still clutched in his hand. "Owen, maybe you should put the gun—"

"You saw Harry kiss me while a video of you played on my phone. I know it looked bad, but that's *perception* not the truth. Think of the data, the evidence. What about Frank and Paul? Lorelei and Tommy? My work. My *home*. Your signature is on every part of the life I've built here. Hours spent just the two of us for months. What probability, what outcome makes more sense? That this was all some elaborate plot to hurt you or just bad timing when once again Harry was trying to hurt *me*?"

The concern in Cal over Owen brandishing the gun melted in place of realization. "And I left you with him…. Owen, I'm so sorry."

"I know." Owen smiled in relief. "I just need you to know that I had nothing to do with that video. Harry sent it to my email and made me watch it. Your client must have given it to him. He wants to use it as blackmail or something, and Harry thought showing it to me would change my opinion of you. It didn't. I'm sorry I watched it. I shouldn't have. But seeing you like that didn't make me think you were… low or less or anything but how I've always seen you.

"I don't care that you're an escort, Cal, but I also can't deny that seeing you with someone else… made me jealous," he admitted, bolstered by the small smile taking shape on Cal's face. "*I* want to touch you like that. But only if you want me to, not because it's business. I...." He could hardly believe he was about to say these next words, but he felt them and needed Cal to know, "I love you. And I'm sure you've heard that a million times—"

"I gave up all my clients."

"What?" Owen blinked at him.

"I quit this morning. The clients I had scheduled this week? I didn't sleep with either of them. I didn't want anyone else to touch me when all I want is you."

There was a moment where the whole rest of the world fell away and it was just them, inches apart with everything on the table, the arm holding the gun beginning to drop, and all Owen could think about was kissing Cal.

"While all this is fascinatin'"—the mugger spoiled the moment—"I gotta say—"

"You don't get to talk right now," Owen snapped, recentering the gun as he willed his arm not to shake from the strain of keeping the heavy weapon upright.

"I just wanna *say*"—the man held his hands higher—"it's not loaded."

"It.... What?" Owen pulled the gun toward him, then quickly pointed it back at the mugger before he could try anything. "If you think I'm that stupid—"

"I swear, man, just check!"

Owen shared an uncertain look with Cal, but when he had the gun and there were two of them against one man, the worst that could happen if the mugger was lying was that he'd bolt. So Owen pulled the gun in again and checked the magazine.

*Empty.*

"What is *wrong* with you?" He pushed the empty weapon into the mugger's arms and smacked his shoulder for good measure. "Why would you do something like that?"

"You'd prefer it *was* loaded?" the man said, shoving the gun into the back of his jeans. "I wasn't gonna kill somebody for loose change, all right. I'm just in a tight spot. Two hundred dollars short on rent, and my new job doesn't start for a week. My daughter and I are gonna be out on the street, so I got desperate. You wanna scream for the cops now, be my guest." He dropped back to lean against the wall, fully deflated from the confrontational figure he'd been portraying.

Owen considered what the man had said as the rapid fire of his pounding pulse diminished. "You only need two hundred?"

"*Owen.*"

"What?" He glanced at Cal with an innocent shrug.

Cal's expressions had run the gamut tonight, but his look of exasperation was one of Owen's favorites because it always seemed so fond of him too. "You are not giving our mugger cash out of the goodness of your heart."

"I know," he said, more forgiving now that the danger had passed. "I really don't have my wallet. But on Monday the mayor's office is going to announce a gun buyback program. I should have a card…." He started to pat down his slacks, then his suit coat, and finally found the small stack of business cards he'd brought with him. Selecting one, he handed it to the mugger. "Here. Go to the nearest precinct, show them my card, and tell them I gave permission for an early exchange. If anyone questions it, they can call me or the mayor directly."

"The *mayor*?" The man accepted the card with a healthy dose of skepticism. "Shit, hoss, you really are some big shot, huh?"

"Not really. I just have good friends. Though make sure you show the card and explain everything before you pull the gun."

"I ain't stupid," he snorted. "Though all this might point to the contrary. They really gonna give me cash for my piece?"

"I'll make sure of it. The program is two hundred dollars per firearm. Maybe the universe is looking out for you." Owen smiled and couldn't help the way his eyes strayed to Cal again.

"That'd be a first, but I ain't complainin'." The man tucked the business card away and pulled the hood from his head. He had a wicked scar down his right eye, but his hair was neatly buzzed and his facial hair trimmed like he was usually more kempt. Not a criminal, just a desperate man taking advantage of so many other criminals moving through these streets.

Hopefully the various pieces to Owen's police program would help do away with that and make things better for everyone in Atlas City.

The man gestured between Owen and Cal. "Whatever mess you two tryin' to work through, good luck. He obviously ain't someone you wanna let get away."

Cal was less accepting of someone who'd tried to rob them, but he nodded as he finally put away his wallet. "I'm starting to remember that."

**JUMPING** to conclusions wasn't Cal's way. He always took his time, checked every angle, *planned*, but seeing Owen with Harrison seemingly kissing, along with the video playing on Owen's phone, had blindsided him, and he hadn't been able to recognize the truth.

Owen was no con artist. Goodness was sewn into the lining of his skin, even enough for him to offer pity to someone who'd attacked them. Most people weren't like that, but most people weren't *Owen Quinn*.

A dangerous alley where they'd already been mugged once was not the appropriate place to share a kiss. They needed to get back to the gala. Owen would be missed, and someone needed to do something about Harrison and his ulterior motives.

Their would-be mugger walked with them the few blocks to the venue—real criminals were less likely to confront *three* men out in the open. When he parted ways with them, he gave his name, "Anton Ramirez," and shook Owen's hand.

Only Owen could have managed such an ending.

If he hadn't been an integral part of the evening's schedule, Cal would have whisked him away right then so they could talk, specifically about the three impossible words Owen had said.

*I love you.*

He loved Cal. And he'd said it freely. Owen was wrong; Cal did not hear that all the time. Normal clients didn't think of him that way. In fact, Cal could count on one hand how many people had ever said those words to him, and one of them was his sister.

After giving his jacket back to the confused coat check attendant, they reentered the ballroom and scanned the area for any sign of Merlin—who appeared to have left—then Harrison, who headed toward them the moment he saw Owen.

Moving swiftly, they in turn sought out Mayor King. Keri stood at his side along with Adam and his wife. The two CEOs were preparing to make a speech about the joint venture and appeared thrilled to see Owen since they'd seen him rush out.

Owen wasted no time explaining why he'd run, all without implicating Cal in anything illegal. Harrison had ambushed him, admitted to starting the rumors about Owen's character, and came here to pull Owen back into his clutches. While the collaboration with Orion Labs should move forward, Harrison's involvement had to end.

Cal expected the fierce expressions Keri and Adam soon wore—he'd already seen how much the pair doted on Owen—but the mayor's severe face was far more intimidating.

"I'll take care of it, Owen. You just enjoy the evening."

While Keri, Adam, and Owen ascended a small platform in the center of the room, the mayor's bodyguards held Harrison back, ensuring he didn't get anywhere near Owen, and escorted him from the ballroom without making a scene. For a moment, Cal wondered about those cement shoes he and Owen had joked about, but he doubted the mayor would go that far.

Watching Owen up there getting the attention and credit he deserved made Cal so proud. This phenomenal man *loved* him. And Cal knew as he looked on from the crowd that he loved Owen just as fiercely.

"He sure is pretty, I'll give ya that."

Cal startled at the sound of his friend's voice. *Rhys* had snuck up on him, wearing his own tux to fit in with the crowd. "How—"

"*Doctor*, remember?" he said, and when he leaned away, Cal noticed the woman on his arm. She had a willowy figure and slighter stature, especially while standing next to a man as burly as Rhys. Her formfitting gown in shades of blue and silver looked like a winter night sky.

"You're Cal," she said, extending a hand.

"And you're *Frost*." He took it gladly.

She laughed. "He's not allowed to call me that anymore."

"How 'bout Snowflake, doll?" Rhys pressed a kiss to the side of her head, and the way she leaned into it told Cal all he needed to know. "Your boy is somethin' else, huh?"

Cal turned back to the platform where the announcement filled the room, with Owen currently at the center. But it was ending, and soon he'd return to Cal. "That he is. But if you'll excuse me." He turned back to take the woman's hand once more and kissed it in goodbye. "We'll have to properly get to know each other another time."

"Double date?" Rhys winked at him.

Lorelei and Tommy, as well as Frank and Paul, weren't far away across the ballroom. "Maybe even a dinner party," Cal said. "But right now, I need to spirit my companion away." The room erupted in applause as Cal headed to the platform to intercept Owen's departure.

"Have fun, buddy!" Rhys called after him.

Cal didn't know about *that*. He hoped they would, that certain things he'd been fantasizing about might come to fruition, but he'd never expect anything from Owen.

Now that Owen's responsibilities were over, when Cal suggested they slip away, he welcomed it, and they caught a cab outside to leave the gala in the rearview mirror. Cal shouldn't have been so nervous the closer they got to Owen's apartment. There were unspoken promises in every glance they stole of each other, but they couldn't have the several intimate conversations they were due in the back of a cab.

Once they were inside the building, however, heading up the elevator, Cal had to ask, "Is that interview going to go differently on Monday?"

"It is. But I'll discuss it with Adam and Keri first. Orion Labs deserves a heads-up too, or they might pull out of the deal themselves. They'll have to do damage control once it's made public that their CTO dated an employee for four years and broke his arm when he tried to leave him." Owen said it all with conviction, but the damaged man he'd been for so long hadn't healed all his fissures yet.

"It's the right thing, Owen."

"I know. I'm almost glad all this happened tonight. For the first time"—a bright smile proved he was finally basking in the pride of everything he'd accomplished as the elevator opened—"I don't feel afraid of anything."

A flash of paranoia stirred in Cal, and he wondered if they'd find Harrison waiting outside Owen's door, but fate was back in their favor. *Freedom* was a good look on Owen.

"Maybe pull back on the heroics when guns are involved next time," Cal said.

"Don't worry." Owen chuckled. "If I hadn't been 100 percent certain I could do it without anyone getting hurt, I wouldn't have."

"Glad those training sessions paid off. Maybe I could use some. Future date with a pair of sisters?"

A more boisterous laugh replied. "Deal."

The quiet, dark apartment enveloped them like a warm embrace when they stepped inside. Owen turned on the main light but kept the rest off, leaving the mood soft and dim. As they removed their coats and hovered near the door, the anticipation of what to do next was worse than any time before it.

"Cal?" Owen whispered.

"Yes?"

"Since I'm not afraid anymore, I don't want to spend another moment *not* kissing you."

Owen brought his hands up to grasp either side of Cal's face, and as he leaned forward and their lips touched, Cal brought his hands up to cover Owen's, rekindling what they'd started the other night.

Owen's warmth made Cal quiver—the slow slide of their tongues, that feeling of completion that had been interrupted the first time. Cal dropped his hands to Owen's wrists but held on as they kissed, and *kissed*, and eventually had to gasp for air, allowing their foreheads to fall together.

"Would you like to get out of these tuxes, Owen?"

"Y-yes."

The exchange was so reminiscent of their first night, Cal didn't want to presume that any more than cuddling was on the table, but he needed to know what was allowed. He stroked Owen's cheek and pressed another firm and then deeper and *deeper* kiss to that lovely mouth, before he spoke again.

"If you're not sure, not ready, we don't have to do anything more than this tonight. If this and our usual routine is all you want, that's enough for me."

"And if it's *not* all I want?"

Cal's chest fluttered from the certainty in Owen's gaze. "Then more sounds wonderful."

Replying with an impish grin, Owen backed toward the bedroom, leading Cal by the hand.

The fluttering turned into a full-on flip of Cal's stomach. He was nervous. He couldn't remember the last time he'd been *nervous*. Once again, Owen thrilled him simply by being *Owen*, the culmination of everything Cal had been missing in life but hadn't understood or been able to accept until he found it.

"I want you to know everything I plan to do to you before I do it," Owen said, "so you can tell me if it's what you want too."

Usually, Cal was the one saying those words. "And what do *you* want?"

Hands up by his bow tie to undo it, that impish smile returned before Owen tugged the bow loose. "I want to undress you. *Everything* this time. And then… ."—ah, *there* was Cal's Scarlet—"…th-then… I want my mouth on you. Would you like that?"

"*Yes.*"

With his smile ever widening, Owen began undoing the buttons to his shirt. Cal would have followed suit, but he could hardly refuse the request for Owen to do the undressing for him, which meant Cal had the luxury of watching Owen disrobe first. Once his companion recognized the inherent role reversal, he grasped Cal's hands to lead him to the bed and sat him on the edge.

Cal had always delighted in Owen's lean lines and smoothly defined muscle tone, but it was different now, better, knowing he'd get to touch everything his eyes took in as Owen finished opening his shirt and dropped that and his jacket from his shoulders.

Flush with color and all for Cal, he lost the tuxedo pants next, so beautiful in only his underwear. The first thing Owen reached for when he stepped between Cal's parted legs was the glasses perched on his nose.

"I want mine on a bit longer, but is this okay?" Owen asked, pulling them from Cal's face. "I love you in them, I just don't want to wreck them."

"I can see well enough without them."

"Good. I wish the first time I saw you bare hadn't been on that video," he added with a grimace.

"Doesn't matter now. Here, our enemies can't touch us. But *you* can touch whatever you like."

A giggle replaced Owen's distress like a slate wiped clean. "I want to kiss you again. Can I?"

"Always."

Taking hold of Cal's face like before, Owen crawled into his lap and teased his tongue along his lips before sliding inside. Cal wasn't used to this dynamic, having someone make it all about him.

"Oh shit." Owen pulled back with a start.

"What is it?"

"I don't have any condoms."

Well that answered the question of how Owen wanted the evening to proceed. "I do. In my wallet. Not an expectation, just habit. Which I'll try to stop saying so much." He grimaced himself this time.

"It's okay. It is *all* okay."

Finding the end of Cal's bow tie, Owen carefully untied it, deft fingers never once fumbling as they moved on to undo his shirt buttons. Cal shouldn't have assumed Owen would be timid in the bedroom. He liked that the confidence Owen usually lacked, he found here, or maybe part of that was because his partner was Cal.

The eager fan of Owen's hands over Cal's chest and down his stomach promised of everything to come, his tux and all its pieces soon dropping to the floor, save the item liberated from Cal's wallet. Then Owen was falling to his knees between Cal's thighs and tugging down his shorts. He barely got them down Cal's calves before his eyes fluttered upward and he leaned forward to taste Cal like he wanted.

Cal's hands went straight for Owen's hair, the well-gelled locks mussing with the barest carding of his fingers and light tugs. Owen hummed at the attention, and the vibrations from the act went straight to the base of Cal's spine. Clients almost never did this for him, but he knew now that he never wanted another mouth on him ever again or different hands gripping his thighs for leverage.

Continuing to pet and praise Owen, Cal let himself relax into the freedom of not needing to perform, because with Owen, he could simply be himself.

As one of Owen's hands slid up Cal's stomach, the other assisting the attentions of his mouth, Cal dropped back on the bed. Owen pushed forward at the invitation to spread Cal's legs wider, getting even closer, and Cal could hardly stand how near to the edge he was already.

"Owen… which of us… is wearing this?" he plucked the condom from the bed.

"*You*."

"Then you better hold off… or I won't last much longer. Tell me." He looked at Owen with every ounce of adoration he felt for him. "How do you want this to go?"

Owen licked his lips and slid his clothed hips against Cal's naked skin as he crawled up his body. "Like our first night, but the way you would have done things if I hadn't stopped you. *Show* me"—he bucked forward as he lay atop Cal—"what you wanted to do to me then."

"On the bed," Cal gasped, certain he had no ability to move unless Owen released him. Then Owen did, dropping onto his feet to stand while he gripped the edge of his underwear.

"*No*, those stay on to start. We have this." Cal held up the condom. "What about other supplies?"

"Bottom drawer." Owen nodded at the nightstand.

Cal went for it, while Owen clambered onto the bed to throw the sheets aside. Once they were ready, Cal placed the items they'd need later within easy reach and settled behind Owen like they'd been so many weeks, *months* now, in the past.

**CAL** was hard. Of course he was; Owen was too. But tonight he could feel skin against the back of his thighs.

Pushing against the body behind him, he felt Cal's hand coil around his waist, tease at his waistband, and dip beneath the elastic. The first brush of fingers made him whimper. Owen had always been noisy, and for Cal he loved that because he wanted him to know how good this felt.

"This is what I would have done," Cal whispered, "but only if you'd asked first. Tell me what you want, Owen. Tell me how to touch you."

It had been so *long*, and Harrison was never like this, always cared for his own pleasure more, while Cal fell into sync with everything Owen asked for.

"Slower," he said, gripping Cal's hand to guide him. In the past, he'd always given in to the whims of his partner. This, finally, was the exchange he'd longed for, where every stroke of Cal's hand mirrored the waves of Owen's body rocking against him. "*Cal....*" He whined before long, and Cal knew without elaboration what he wanted.

Only then did Owen's underwear get torn away, and the slick slide of a new connection brought out louder noises from his throat. Minutes of careful attention passed to make sure he was prepared, before Cal shifted to take the connection deeper.

"Ready?" He asked permission first.

"Yes," Owen said with a sharp intake of breath. "Please...."

With the linking of their bodies, Owen gripped Cal's wrist to connect them further while Cal reached once more between his thighs. They sought an end together, and when they found it, overlapping and breathless, all Owen wanted was to keep Cal close, even arching his neck around to steal a kiss. Disentangling was even better, because it meant he could kiss Cal properly, with the same passion as if they could start all over again.

"Insatiable, are you?" Cal said, low and sultry against his lips.

"For you? Always."

It might have been the rush of endorphins, the high of a first time, but Owen didn't care. He wanted to revel in this feeling for the rest of the night.

Once they were cleaned up enough to lie comfortably with the covers pulled around them, snuggling the way they used to felt miles different. Owen couldn't stop smiling. His cheeks hurt from the strain, because Cal's fingers were laced with his, legs tangled, nothing between them but skin. There was too much to smile about, especially when Cal kept pressing kisses to his temple, cheek, and lips.

"There are several serious things we should talk about," Cal said when it seemed like they might lounge and kiss and exist that way forever.

"Like what?"

"Like... what if, after tonight, I really was your publicist?"

"For real?" Owen exclaimed. "Would you like that? Could we do that?"

"The way I see it, we simply need to work out a reasonable salary, a fair job description of tasks for me to complete, and we're already halfway there. *If* you like the idea. Imagine there's an event you don't want to deal with," Cal said with a teasing grin. "You can make an appearance as needed, but then your *publicist* might have to whisk you away for another engagement—which may or may not lead to inappropriate behavior in a limousine."

Owen giggled, but he could tell Cal was edgy offering this. "So I'd still be paying you to stick around?"

"No. You'd be paying me to do something I enjoy. I'd stick around after hours because I want to. Unless that's too weird for you—"

"*No.* I like it. But are you sure? I still can't believe you quit for me."

"It's what I want," Cal said. "If you hadn't noticed, I rather enjoy being your publicist, and I am *fantastic* at it."

"You are," Owen said with another snicker.

"Plus, there is a bonus to the arrangement."

"You mean this?" He tightened his hold on Cal's hand.

"*This* was amazing. But I mean something else." Cal kissed Owen's fingertips, and the blue of his eyes glittered as he said, "I love you, Owen."

"You... *really*?" Owen's heart nearly stuttered to a stop, because *he'd* said it earlier, but he hadn't expected to hear it back.

Cal nodded, but any words he might have spoken were stolen by Owen's kiss.

"Do you know the great thing about data models?" Owen said, quiet and intimate between them. "They make it look like you knew what you were doing all along, even if you just figured things out a few minutes ago. They put everything into perspective, so that even a jumbled past can paint a clear picture of the future. Sometimes that's all we need."

Cal kissed Owen softly in response. "I couldn't have said it better."

"So, umm...." Owen stared at the face scant millimeters from his own. "Want to take a shower, make popcorn, and watch some cheesy sci-fi movie before bed?"

A delighted laugh responded. "I *love* you," Cal said again.

That laugh, those words—Owen would never tire of hearing any of it. "I love you too."

## *Chapter Ten*

**CAL** and Owen had experienced lazy days before, bleeding from one night into another, but Sunday was different than any day before it. Cal didn't have a change of clothes with him, so after they'd showered the night before, he'd stolen one of Owen's T-shirts and sleep pants for their movie. He would have gladly stayed in those clothes indefinitely given the way Owen looked at him while his fingers traced the screen print of the DeLorean from *Back to the Future*.

They couldn't hide from the world forever, though, and eventually, the next day, Cal had to put his clothes back on, sans suit coat and bow tie, and head home. Owen accompanied him.

"Are you sure I'm not imposing?"

A few months ago, he might have been. Cal didn't let people into his home. He didn't let people into his *life*. Owen changed everything. "You're not imposing. Besides, my apartment is closer to Nye Industries for Monday, and I'm hoping you won't want to leave until then."

Owen's smile could have lit up a dark room.

Without argument they retired to Cal's apartment with an overnight bag for Owen. The evening was filled with new ways to explore each other, but soon it was the next morning again and time for life to continue.

"You can come with me," Owen said, scowling at the alarm clock they'd already hit Snooze on twice. "I have to make my session with Lorelei this morning. I want to tell her about Harry. Then I have to tell Frank. Calling Alyssa, Casey, and Mario can't wait forever either, and I should touch base with Keri and Adam before the interview. It's all so... much.

"I mean, I don't need you hanging at my side all day." He glanced away in embarrassment. "But you could come to my training session, then walk me in to work, see the building a little. I know I'll be okay after that. It's weird, though, thinking about telling some stranger what happened to me."

Cal held Owen's hand close to his chest, still awed by being able to lie with Owen like this after so long having to hold back. "*I* was a stranger in the beginning. So was Lorelei. And Frank. I know this is different, but you don't have to sensationalize what happened. Say what needs to be said, what you're comfortable saying, and leave things there. It'll be enough."

"I feel... guilty," Owen said, keeping his eyes on their clasped hands. "I don't think Harrison means to be a bad person."

"Owen...."

"I *know*. I'm doing it again, but... I cared for him once. I'm not being petty, right?" Hazel eyes flicked upward to meet Cal's gaze.

"No. You're being honest. You're protecting yourself. It's been less than a year. You could still file charges for assault if you wanted."

"Oh, I don't know. He'd probably turn around and try to charge me for last night."

"You defended yourself from a previous attacker."

"My word against his."

"Which is entirely different from you having medical records of a broken arm from the real assault," Cal said. "Even if it doesn't stick, the truth will be out there to better protect you and any future partners roped into his clutches." He didn't mean to push; he just tended to get heated when it came to his loved ones.

"You're right," Owen said. "I know you're right. It just feels so much more real again."

"I know, but you are so strong. You didn't only prove that at the gala but for months moving on without him. You are remarkable, Owen. Never let him make you doubt that. As for the rest, Orion Labs will see reason with the venture. If Harrison ends up without a job, excuse me for not shedding any tears." It might have been a cold thing to say, but it broke Owen's somber disposition.

"What about you?" he asked, snuggling closer to Cal instead of untangling like they should. "Merlin and that video?"

Like a fresh trill from the alarm clock, Cal's phone on the nightstand began to ring. *Lara's* name blinked at them.

"Let's find out, shall we?" Stretching back to snag it, Cal answered with a jovial, "You're up early."

"Please, as if you've even slept the past two days despite not leaving the bedroom," she teased.

"We've slept. *And* left the bedroom."

"Oh really? Where are you now?"

Owen stifled a giggle into Cal's shoulder.

"It's seven thirty in the morning," Cal defended. "Any news on Merlin?"

Lara snorted at the change in subject. "You won't have to worry about him."

"What happened?" Owen asked, perking up at Cal's side.

"Marsh and Merlin didn't count on you two being a unified front," she said louder for his benefit. "Now that we have that footage, who could be blackmailed changes. Did you really think he could blow this up as proof of prostitution without making himself culpable? If he so much as breathes wrong in this city, especially in the direction of any escort services, he's the one who'll be prosecuted.

"Not that Dick would ever throw you under the bus by revealing that footage." She dropped some of her teasing edge. "But he certainly made it sound convincing to Merlin."

"Tell him I owe him a fruit basket," Cal said. One of the many reasons he'd been so loyal to Nick of Time was that Dick could be one scary bastard when necessary.

"It'll really be okay?" Owen leaned over Cal to speak into the phone.

"Merlin has no ammunition, Owen," Lara said, "and his bed is going to stay cold for a very long time. You just worry about you and Calvin. And invite me to that next dinner party! I'll bring the wine."

Owen's renewed giggle soothed Cal better than any news about Merlin's downfall. They'd be okay, but first they had to finish taking down Harrison.

After hanging up the call, it was like a day in the life of Owen Quinn—heading into the city to attend his lesson with Lorelei, then his routine on the way to work getting his favorite morning coffee, and finally entering Nye Industries where everyone, security included, showed Owen such deference that Cal felt humbled by how much of the city understood Owen's worth as well as he did.

Owen's support structure was growing, with Lorelei and Frank especially, who both offered bodily harm to Harrison after hearing about Saturday night.

"I'm aware my combat reflexes are next to nil, but I can still *look* intimidating," Frank said. He was sufficiently tall and broad, but Cal would hardly call him intimidating. They'd been stopped by Frank in the hall on their way to see Keri.

"Owen can handle himself quite impressively, as it turns out," Cal said.

Frank smiled with a ready response only to flounder, eyes widening as they focused over Cal and Owen's shoulders. "That's, uhh, good… coz apparently security sucks today."

Cal spun around, already anticipating who they'd find before his eyes landed on Harrison headed toward them. The man's severe expression had Cal prepared to step in front of Owen to protect him, but Owen pulled Cal behind him first.

"Owen, if you don't want—"

"I got this. Frank, alert Keri and security for me, will you?"

"If you're sure," Frank said and backed up before turning tail to rush the opposite direction.

The loathing Cal felt for Harrison didn't need any encouragement. When Owen first told him the story of what happened, Cal had pictured his father. He saw the similarities in the men clearly in person, not in appearance, but in the foundation of their sneers, like they believed they had a right to whatever they wanted no matter who got hurt along the way. That Owen could stand up to Harrison now was a sign of how far he'd come.

"You're pushing me out?" Harrison said, stopping closer to Owen than Cal liked. "All this put at risk, and for what? *Him*?"

Owen touched Cal's arm as he kept him guarded behind him. "If Orion Labs is willing to shift ownership of the venture elsewhere, that doesn't change that we're still moving forward with it. When you first came here, you said you understood if that's what I wanted. But you didn't mean that, did you? You only said it to trick me, and when I didn't act the way you wanted, you shed your skin like the *snake* you are."

Instead of anger, the lie of sympathetic pleading surged up in Harrison. Cal saw now who the real con artist was. "You don't see the danger in fraternizing with someone like him? Given your position, your career?"

"After the things you've done to me, you dare—"

"I *love* you, Owen." He stepped closer, causing Owen to back up and draw Cal back with him. "I always have. I only want what's best for you."

"No you don't. You want what's best for you. And that includes having me bow to everything you want. That's not a partnership, Harry, and it's time Orion Labs and everyone else learned what you are."

Harrison's carefully constructed mask flickered. "Are you threatening me?"

"You threatened *me*. You threatened *Cal*. I'm just telling the truth."

"Are you now?" he huffed, gesturing widely at the office space beyond the hallway. "All these people know what your *publicist* really is? Have you been truthful about that?"

Heads had started popping up from surrounding cubicles and out of office doorways, creating the exact scene Harrison wanted, assuming he could grab the upper hand if only he cornered Owen again.

"You started those rumors to discredit me," Owen fought back, "to force me into thinking I needed you, and you expect me to thank you for that? To run back into your arms? With you, I could have been anyone. You never cared about me. You wanted someone who was easy to control. But you were never enough for me, Harry, and you never will be."

"So you have to *pay for it* instead?" he barked.

That, of course, was when Frank returned with Keri. Cal heard them coming and glanced behind him, only to see that it was more than only two pairs of feet, because Adam and Mayor King were with her.

"I do pay him," Owen said, not knowing how much their audience had grown. "*And* I'm sleeping with him. But I do not pay him to sleep with me. That was never what this was about."

"You expect me to believe that?" Harrison scoffed. "He's a *prostitute*."

That word carried enough weight for Cal to feel the scrutiny of the many eyes on him, but Owen didn't falter. "You can think whatever you want." He reached back to take Cal's hand. "I'm happy. It's a shame you only know how to make a partner miserable. You were never worth the effort I put into you, and it feels good to finally get that."

"Owen," the mayor spoke as the initial voice of authority. Owen turned, stepping to the side to accept the new additions to their circle, while King spared an icy glance at Harrison. "I see you have things handled. The three of us feared you might need additional support today. Pity we were right."

"Mr. Marsh," Keri addressed Harrison directly, "security is on its way to escort you from the building. I trust you won't resist."

Even Adam, who Cal had come to think of as an overlarge puppy, looked menacing, with Frank holding back like witnessing a slow-motion car crash.

Recognizing that he was vastly outnumbered, Harrison scrambled for something, anything to reclaim the conversation. "Owen, you're making a mistake. You—"

"No." He shot down the man who he'd worked so hard to put behind him. "My mistake was you. Now I'm moving on."

Cal saw the rage spring to life on Harrison's face like the fuse of an explosive lit, but Owen turned to depart through his circle of friends and didn't notice. The expression was familiar to Cal, so when Harrison lurched forward, wild and angry, he was ready to intercept.

He gripped Harrison's wrist before the man could grab Owen's and used his hold as leverage to power a fierce punch across Harrison's jaw. When he let go, Harrison stumbled, dazed. Cal's hand stung, but it was worth it to see that bastard topple.

"Better watch that temper, *Harry*. It'll get you into more trouble than you know."

A spattering of applause sounded from the spectators—even Frank let out a laugh that he stifled with his hand—but while Keri, Adam, and the mayor stood stoic, Owen's reaction was all Cal cared about, and he looked so moved that even if he didn't need rescuing, Cal was there to watch his back.

Cal reached for Owen's hand that had been rudely ripped away when he stepped in to stop Harrison's lunge.

"H-he assaulted me!" Harrison sputtered.

"Not the way it looked from our angle, Mr. Marsh," Keri said, crossing her arms and nodding curtly at security as they finally arrived from down the hall.

They swarmed Harrison and lifted him from the ground.

"Wait!" he tried, but no one was listening to him anymore.

In short order, he was carted away, leaving Owen holding gratefully to Cal's hand, while he looked at the three powerful figures who'd become his friends, at Frank who'd become a *dear* friend, and at their audience, who was starting to return to work.

As strong as Owen had been while facing Harrison, he was still reserved deep down and hunched in on himself now that the commotion was over. "About what Harrison said—"

"Your personal life is your own, Owen," Adam interrupted, smiling congenially again. "If you found love with your… *publicist*, well that's just good fortune since you spend so much time together."

"You're welcome to stay through the interview, Mr. White," Keri added, "and as long as you'd like after that."

It was obvious to Cal, in the case of Mayor King in particular, that they knew there was truth to what Harrison had accused them of, but they respected Owen too much to care.

"I think I will stay," Cal said, looking to Owen beside him. "If you'd like that?"

"Yes. Thank you. Thank *you*," he said again to the people who'd come together for his sake, Frank included. "And if it's all right with everyone, since I have all of you here… I'd like to tell you what I plan to say in that interview."

**EVERYTHING** had a pattern. The trick to understanding the data was in the models. The algorithms. The points along a timeline that indicated the probability of what should come next.

Owen's whole world revolved around patterns, but some things couldn't be predicted. Whenever that happened, he thought back to something his mother once told him.

"Meet every surprise in life like you had a plan all along."

Owen still didn't have a plan. But he was starting to be okay with that. Some things he could predict, he'd built his entire career off that, but the rest would work itself out with time and effort and the belief that he was finally fighting for what he wanted.

Next he had to get through introducing Cal to his family.

His adopted father Doug, Alyssa, and Casey were coming for a visit, with Mario tagging along. Cal's sister, Claire, was coming too. They'd had several dinner parties over the past few weeks since the interview made Owen's personal life public—adding Lara, Cal's friend Rhys, and his girlfriend Danielle to the usual suspects. Even Keri and Wesley, and Adam and Teresa attended a few. But this was the first time their loved ones from Middleton would all be in the same room.

Orion Labs had fired Harrison in the aftermath of the scandal, but they appreciated the heads-up Keri gave them before the story went live and happily continued the partnership with a new representative sent to work in Atlas City.

Harrison would likely get a new job eventually, once the scandal died down, though Owen tried not to think about it. Sometimes he'd catch himself wondering what Harrison was up to, if coming clean had been the right thing, but then he'd look at Cal, at his apartment, at the life he'd built here and remember why he'd put Harrison behind him in the first place. He deserved to be happy and *here* was where he'd found it.

Merlin hadn't shown his face since, not in any circles that mattered. Life moved on, and Owen moved forward, for once feeling safe and excited for what came next, even amid the unexpected.

"What do you mean *hack* the nanomachines?" he said, busying himself in the kitchen, while Cal organized the counter.

"I mean, if this project with Nye and Walker revolves around chip technology and nanomachines for gene therapy... what happens if someone hacks the program? Could they manipulate the amount of medication being given or the direction the gene therapy takes? Cause irreparable damage maybe? Even make someone devolve into a monkey?"

Owen snorted. "Okay, *King Koopa*. Now you're thinking like a supervillain. Although...." The inner working of Owen's mind buzzed with probability. "I should probably make sure that's not possible."

Now it was Cal who laughed, obviously having only meant to tease Owen, but it got him thinking. There was always more to consider, more work to be done, and Cal inspired Owen and led him down paths he never expected. Challenging each other, bringing out the best in each other, that's how a relationship was supposed to work. It amazed Owen sometimes that he'd never realized that until he had it.

Everything was ready now for their families to arrive. Dinner waiting, the apartment spotless, any items of Cal's that had matriculated into Owen's home displayed proudly. Cal still had his apartment, but they rarely spent nights apart. If they managed to avoid disaster tonight—even if they didn't—Owen planned to ask Cal to move in with him over breakfast tomorrow.

While Cal finished setting out the wine and beer glasses for initial drinks to break the tension, Owen walked across the apartment to turn on some background music. The first song that started was Ella Fitzgerald singing "Someone to Watch Over Me"—just like the night they met.

Owen smiled, eyes closing as he hummed along and swayed in place. A few seconds later, when fingers alighted on his wrist, tentative but surer in their grip when Owen didn't flinch, the world seemed to have come full circle as he was spun about and pulled into Cal's body for a dance.

"Hey—" he started to protest.

"*I* am wearing shoes. *You* are not. Therefore, at the moment, *I'm* taller," Cal said, continuing to lead with an arm around Owen's waist. "Besides, this way I can finally prove to you that I am more than two left feet."

A giggle left Owen as he gave in, well trained in how to be the partner who followed, but with Cal, he could be both, he could be *everything*, including himself.

The steps didn't matter before long, just the touch of Cal's hand guiding him, their fingers clasped and held between them, and Owen's head falling forward to rest on Cal's shoulder. Again, he hummed and eventually began to sing along.

"You have a lovely voice, you know."

"Really? I was always too shy to sing in front of people."

"Given your new lease on life, I'd say that calls for karaoke this weekend."

"Oh no!" Owen pulled up with a laugh. "Don't tell Mario that. He'll *insist*. But it would probably be fun. Gotta keep everyone entertained while they're here, right?"

Cal led Owen across the floor, faster and faster into a twirl, where he spun Owen outward and back in against him for a low dip that made Owen giggle that much harder.

"I cave," he said. "You are much better at this when you know the steps."

"See? But I don't mind it the other way." Cal proceeded into a slower sway again. "You'll just have to teach me more, Scarlet."

That sounded wonderful. Everything sounded wonderful when Cal called him Scarlet. "Remember now, no matter what Doug says once they get here, if he tries to do the whole passive-aggressive 'you're not good enough for my son' bit, he's just like that, he means well, and he will not sway my opinion."

Nothing but confidence shone on Cal's face. "I'm not worried. He's going to love me. My age notwithstanding, I am not Harrison, and all he'll need to see to understand that is how happy you are and how much I love you. You are happy, aren't you, Owen?" He brushed a stray hair from Owen's forehead.

"More than I've ever been, because I love you too."

They kissed, softly, intimately, and swayed awhile longer, well into the next song. Owen thought to himself like he had the night Harrison first breezed into his life again that he'd never really loved Harry because he hadn't known what love felt like until now.

A chime from Cal's phone reminded them that there wasn't much time before company arrived. They kissed once more before Cal moved to retrieve it from the kitchen counter.

He snorted when he read the message. "Apparently, Claire ran into your family on the metro. She recognized Alyssa. They've been getting to know each other at Impulse, you know."

"I know." Owen crossed the room to join him. "I kind of love that. Did she say anything else?"

Cal turned the phone toward him so he could read the end of the message.

*Why didn't you tell me Owen had a hot single friend?*

"Is she talking about *Mario*?"

"This should be fun." Cal chuckled. "Ready?"

It was such a simple question for a major turning point, but Owen had an equally simple answer. "Yes. Some things you can't predict, but when that happens—"

"Pretend you had a plan all along," Cal finished, reaching for Owen's fingers to draw them to his mouth and kiss his knuckles.

Owen smiled at how well Cal knew him, how well he listened, how well he fit into this wonderful mess of a life they shared. "Exactly."

A few minutes later, just like their first night together, the next stage in their lives began with a knock at the door.

# *Coming in April 2019*

## Dreamspun Desires #79
### Yes, Chef by T. Nielson

A savory slice of first love.

Simon's dad died when he was young, leaving Simon to take the reins of the family restaurant business—and the responsibility for his mother and brothers. His commitment to his duty left Simon time for little else, least of all romance.

Argentinian celebrity chef Luke Ferreya has wanted Simon since their culinary-school days, but for Simon, family always came first. Now Luke's back in Simon's life—briefly before he returns to South America—and he's determined to give Simon a sample of everything he's missed out on.

Simon's brothers are grown, and his mother is doing fine on her own, and Luke is offering a second chance for a future full of the pleasures of fine food, wine, and especially love. Without his obligations to hide behind, can Simon finally allow himself to say "Yes, Chef"?

## Dreamspun Desires #80
### Under His Protection by LaQuette

They can escape their enemies, but not the desire between them.

Prosecutor Camden Warren is on the fast track to professional nirvana. With his charm, his sharp legal mind, and his father as chief judge in the highest court in NY, he can't fail. Nothing can derail his rise to the top... until an attempt on his life forces him to accept the help of a man he walked out on five years ago.

Wounded in the line of duty, Lieutenant Elijah Stephenson wants to ride his new desk job until retirement—not take a glorified babysitting gig with more risk than it's worth... especially not protecting the entitled lawyer who disappeared after the best sex of their lives.

The threat against Camden's life is real, but their passion for each other might prove the greatest danger they've yet to face.